GREY LANCE

GREY
LANCE

by

GERALD
RAFTERY

illustrated by
MARGERY GILL

THE BODLEY HEAD

Illustrations © The Bodley Head Ltd 1960
Printed and bound in Great Britain for
THE BODLEY HEAD LTD
10 Earlham Street, London, w.c.2
by Lowe and Brydone (Printers) Ltd, London
First published in Great Britain 1952
This edition 1960

CONTENTS

For
EARLE and
ERIC HILL

I. A WOLF IS TRAPPED

THE three wolves, worn and thin with winter, turned southward before the driving snow. The bitter wind pressed their low-hung tails against their legs, and they looked like beaten dogs as they drifted before the moaning gale.

And they were beaten. The rangy black father, the white mother, and the gaunt young grey were all that remained of the family of five. Two months back, at the end of December, they had pulled down a moose after a long week's chase. It had begun their bad luck; one fierce slash of a hoof had split the skull of one of the cubs.

The moose had been the last big game they had run down. The dry summer before had driven the huge animals southward, and through the bitterest weeks of winter the little pack had caught only a stray rabbit or a fluffy ptarmigan, that was more feathers than meat.

Now the survivors were lean and starving. Two weeks ago the second cub had failed to wake after a bitter night when the wind had driven the temperature down to fifty degrees below zero. Now with nothing in their bellies but moss and bark, the three wolves headed southward and eastward away from their range. Hunger, sharper than the wind and harsher than the frost, drove them on their way.

All night they padded along in single file with a full moon occasionally breaking through the whirling snow to cast their shadows beside them. It was a true blizzard; not a flake fell from the cloudless sky, but the whining wind picked up the powdery snow and spun it in a blinding cloud until it stung like blown sand.

The dawn found them entering a stretch of wooded country, and the wind went down as the sun came up. The grey yearling was uneasy among the huge trees. His short life had been spent on the open tundra and these huge trees, masked with snow, seemed dangerous. But he followed his father and mother, as untiring as they and as fiercely hungry.

Two days and nights they travelled through the forest, with only a few hours' rest in the lee of a snow-drift, or a snatched mouthful of bitter moss or stinging snow to keep them going. Then their luck changed.

They had passed by night over a range of hills as cold and lifeless as mountains on the moon. There was not a trail to be seen or scented, not the punched track of a rabbit nor the lacy footprints of a mouse. No life stirred or breathed in all that frozen waste.

Even the iron-muscled black wolf was beginning to tire and weaken; his pace slowed and the other two were more than willing to slacken their speed. At dawn they padded into a little clearing, and their leader suddenly stopped dead in his tracks.

For long minutes he stood like a frozen, frost-tipped statue. Only his eyes moved, and the questioning tip of his nose. Gradually the steaming plumes of his breath came more slowly. He began to step softly backward, his huge paws moving lightly back into the tracks he had made. The white wolf moved back, too, and the grey yearling could see that she trembled with eagerness. He looked at the drifted snow of the clearing and saw nothing unusual on its wind-smoothed surface.

Twenty, thirty feet the wolves backed along the way they had come. Then they began to stalk the clearing; delicately, in a half crouch, the black father and the white mother circled the open space. Slowly they worked their way to a little rise that overlooked the open glade.

At the very edge the black wolf stopped and crouched in the snow. The white one crept up beside him until her head was at his shoulder. He began to rock softly back and forth like a cat about to spring, his paws testing the footing. Then he launched forward in a great leap, to land with his head thrust deep into the snow. A split second behind him, the white wolf jumped.

The clearing exploded into sound as half a dozen partridges burst into full flight from their shelter beneath the powdery snow. Like feathered rockets they fled into the air, and left one of their number dead behind them, where the black wolf's leap had trapped it. Another flapped wildly with one wing gripped in the white wolf's teeth. She dragged it back to earth, planted both forepaws on its struggling body, and clipped off its head with one snap of her jaws.

The two winter-thin birds were little enough for three starving wolves and they did not waste a morsel. Every bone was crunched and swallowed; every blood-stained flake of snow was nosed out and greedily gulped down.

The food gave their gaunt bodies new energy, and for three days they hunted through the silent aisles of the wooded hills. Never again did they catch the slight air-hung scent of the birds, or glimpse the faint grey shadows under the snow that showed their roosting places.

They gave up the search and headed southward again. Two days later, the black wolf halted at the edge of a clearing. Before them stood an abandoned cabin; the broken door hung open, and drifted snow heaped the floor. The white wolf whined in uneasiness, but the giant black sniffed the wind carefully and sank back on the snow to watch. Only hunger could have kept him so close to a haunt of man.

In a few minutes something stirred and scratched inside the cabin. The three waited with ears turned alertly toward the sound. A half an hour, an hour passed. A faint gnawing and an odd rattling sound came to them from time to time.

Finally a slow-footed porcupine came waddling out of the door. The fear of man and his works was strong in the wolves, and they did not stir from their places until the clumsy animal had left the clearing. Then they closed in on him, the father growling a fierce warning to the grey yearling to keep his distance from the prickly little beast.

The porcupine lashed his tail back and forth desperately, but the wolves kept closing in, circling and growling. Then the white wolf stepped forward. Carefully she thrust her forepaw deep into the snow beneath him; with a deft stroke she turned him helpless upon his back. With her teeth bared and her lips drawn far up, she gave one delicate slash of her fangs at the trunk muscles which helped the porcupine curl up tight.

It was not a feast, but it was food, and they carefully ate all but the needles.

Three days later, and a hundred miles farther south, their hunger drove them into a deed of far greater daring.

It was the sound that first attracted them, a strange growling and scuffling noise in a snow-filled gully. Slowly they crept through the brush to a point where they could see what was happening. A big grey fox was caught in a trap by one foot. Busily and with evident pain, he was gnawing off his own foot to escape. Grimly the three wolves watched and waited. The scent of iron was enough to make them keep their distance, and the actual sight of the trap and the chain which bound it to a clog reinforced the warning.

Finally the fox broke free and hobbled into the brush toward them. The black wolf backed cautiously away, and only when the crippled animal reached the ground that the wolves had already trod in safety, did the father lead a rush that bore the fox down before he could utter a bark.

The meal revived the little pack. When nothing remained of the fox but the bare skull and scattered bits of fur, the black wolf nosed carefully up and down the gully. A hundred yards away he found the uncovered snowshoe tracks of the trapper; they were cold and almost scentless. Satisfied, he led his little family back into the hills for rest and sleep.

At noon the next day Jean-Louis Lalibert came by with his dog, making his twice-weekly circuit of his thirty-mile trap line. He stared angrily at the remains of the unlucky fox and growled out a string of heartfelt French oaths. His dog growled as heartily as he, and the trapper cursed him, too.

Scratching his three-months' beard in puzzlement, Jean-Louis went carefully over the ground, building up in his mind the picture of what had happened. When he came to the tracks of the wolves he called forth some new and special oaths, reserved for great occasions, and unslung his rifle in careful haste to check its condition.

Then he reached down and patted Gros-Gros in apology; he had done well to growl so fiercely.

This called for some deep thinking; the trapper squatted down on his heels and stuffed his pipe with rank home-grown tobacco. There had been many wolves in his father's day and in his grandfather's; he had heard long tales around the fire at night about their fierceness and their cunning. He must remember now, and out of his father's experience he must make a plan. Jean-Louis was wise in the ways of fox and mink and fisher and marten, but wolves were a new problem.

The shadows of the short winter afternoon were lengthening when he knocked out the bitter ashes of his fourth pipe. He had a plan; it was built out of the wisdom of his Great-uncle Baptiste who had once guarded a deer carcass from wolves with a bit of iron chain laid across it, of a man in Ungava in '98 who had scared a wolf with an oil lantern, and of a half-breed he had met once in Trois Pistoles who had lost two dogs of a sledge team to raiding wolves in the Barren Ground.

He tramped out of the gully into the open valley. There was a thick spruce patch five hundred yards away within clear view of the spot where he stood. He chopped down four saplings and stripped them to poles, then made a rough fence of them around a small tree. On one corner he hung the looted trap, on another a piece of clog chain, on a third his pipe, and on the fourth his grimy bandanna handkerchief.

Then he led Gros-Gros into the centre and tied him to the tree. He knelt in the snow and took the dog's head between his hands; gravely he explained the plan to him, and assured him that there was no danger.

This done, Jean-Louis tramped off down the valley, assuring himself, too, that there was no danger. He, a veteran of Vimy Ridge, should fear nothing. Dragging his sledge along, he paced off the distance. The moon would rise early and it would be a little past full. The light would be good and the wind would blow toward him; it was a good plan.

In the spruce thicket he broke off some branches for a seat. They would keep him off the snow, and they would make a fire if he needed one in a hurry. He set the sights of his rifle for five hundred yards and placed his flashlight on the sledge beside him. That would scare off the wolves if necessary. He settled himself for a long cold wait, chewing peppery strips of jerked venison for his supper.

The sun sank in a grey haze and a cold wind blew up the valley. For two hours there was no sound but the faint moan of the light wind through the spruce branches. A light began to show on the eastern ridge and the moon slipped slowly upward through the trees.

Ink-black shadows on the white snow crept slowly back to their trees as the moon rose. The lonely Gros-Gros, down in the valley, lifted his nose to the shining disk and gave a long howl. He was cold and hungry and lost, and he put all his feeling into the wail.

Half a mile back in the hills, the three wolves were stirring themselves from sleep when they heard the sound. The young grey sat back on his haunches and gave an answering howl.

Jean-Louis in his spruce thicket snapped full awake from a chilly doze. He worked his stiffened fingers inside his fur mittens and got softly to his feet. He rubbed his eyes and set his rifle in the crotch of a tree.

Ten minutes later Gros-Gros gave a series of wild barks and yelps. He saw the lurking forms of the wolves at the edge of the brush.

The grey yearling made a rush forward only to be driven back by his father with stern growls and bared teeth. Slowly the black stalked out into the moonlight, the white wolf at his heels. They trod delicately with quivering muscles, ready to spring back from every spot on which they stepped. The scent of man was strong, but the lure of the dog was stronger. Cautiously they circled the little enclosure at a safe distance, while Gros-Gros yelped with a fury that tried to conceal his fear.

In the spruce patch Jean-Louis slipped off a mitten and hunched over his rifle. He sighted on a clear patch of snow at the left of the pen and waited.

The black wolf circled closer, wrinkling his nose at the scent of man and iron. Suddenly some sense of danger brought him out of the crouch up to his full height. He stared up the valley; he saw the flash, but he never heard the sprawling report. His tensed muscles sent him up in a spring before he collapsed and went down in a lifeless heap on the snow.

The white wolf leaped to his side, snarling defiance at the unseen danger. She glared wildly around while Jean-Louis hastily pumped another shell into the chamber and sighted again. Her white form was outlined against the body of her dead mate as Jean-Louis squeezed off the second shot. Down she went, yelping and kicking in the bloodstained snow. The trapper jacked up another cartridge and burst out of his hiding place, floundering forward on numbed legs.

The maimed wolf was dragging herself toward the line of brush when he stopped and fired a third shot that left her silent and still in the moonlight.

The young grey had sunk down trembling at the first shot, but a feeling that was stronger than fear sent him crawling forward despite the second and third. It was the scent of death that stopped him in his tracks at the edge of the brush. Then Jean-Louis shouted to Gros-Gros, and the young wolf fled quivering, with his tail between his legs.

For an hour he ran, silent and panic-struck, down shadowy aisles of trees and across open moonlit clearings. In wild ten-foot leaps he went over the level snow-covered lakes where the wind-cleared patches of ice showed green-black.

Finally he stopped, exhausted, with heaving flanks and trembling legs. He sank down on the snow and panted in swift sobbing breaths. The world was dark and cold and empty. When dawn came he scratched a nest in the side of a drift and crawled in, tired and shivering.

At moonrise the next night he started on a long, fruitless hunt that ended in another cold and hungry bed. The second night he scratched away the snow and ate some dry frozen moss. The third night he captured a mouse prospecting too far from its nest in a hollow stump.

The following night brought a real victory; a weasel in its winter ermine had just run down a squirrel when the young wolf stumbled upon them. He smothered the weasel's snarls in a flurry of slashes, and then ate the musk-tainted hunter and his prey at leisure. He slept peacefully that day and the strange feeling of loss that had haunted him since the death of his parents was almost gone. It was just before moonrise when he started his hunt and in a few minutes he found a prize. It was a rabbit dead in a snare, dangling three feet above the ground.

He stalked carefully around it twice and found nothing suspicious. He sat on his haunches with lolling tongue and stared up at it. His father and mother had robbed Indians' snares in the dim past; he did not know that they would have been more cautious on Jean-Louis Lalibert's trap line.

Finally he leaped and caught the rabbit in his jaws. Tugging strongly at it, he danced around on his hind legs. One foot skidded on metal, and then—snick! A fox trap slammed shut, high up on his left hind leg.

He forgot the rabbit and made a wild dash for freedom. The chain brought him up short in mid-leap with a ferocious pull on his leg. He turned and, heedless of the smell of iron, scratched and dug wildly into the snow about the clog.

He unearthed the length of wood and sank his teeth savagely into it, swinging and wrestling it loose from the frozen earth. When it rolled free, he tried again to escape. Tugging painfully, he managed to drag the clog a little distance until it snagged on a bush. He scratched it loose and then dragged it, bumping and rolling, a hundred feet farther. The trap had gripped him across the big muscle above the hock and he was able to throw his full weight into the pull.

He rested, panting, and began to overcome the unthinking panic which had gripped him at first. Carefully he tugged the clog into motion and dragged it another hundred feet. There he came upon the tracks of Lalibert, which had been carefully brushed and covered closer to the trap. Wild fear flooded over him at that hated scent. He plunged madly away again and within thirty feet the clog caught and yanked him helpless to the ground. He sat up, shivering and panting. Slowly he fought back the wild desire to fight the clog, to seize the chain with his teeth and shake it. His native intelligence began to come to the surface.

Carefully he rolled the clog free of the brush and then walked the length of the chain before throwing his weight into the pull. He discovered quickly that a slow steady pace was best, and he learned to watch the progress of the clog and steer it away from snags. He sensed that he left a clear trail and his only safety was in distance, so he travelled steadily and as fast as he dared. The day dawned grey and dark but still he toiled on. He came upon a chain of little lakes. There was a bitter wind whipping across them but the going on the snow-covered ice was smooth and easy.

He staggered onward with the clog skating smoothly over the crusted snow and dragging painfully in the drifts. In midmorning the wind died and snow began to fall, but still he toiled on. Not until the sifting snow became a thick white curtain did he feel safe enough to stop. He worked his way to the nearest shore, a natural fear of the ice driving him on, and hollowed a shelter in the lee of a drift. He sank wearily to sleep with the snow piling up about him.

It was late that night when he stirred again. He staggered to his feet and shook off the fleecy snow which was still falling steadily. It was hard work to tug loose the chain and still harder to scratch the clog out of the snow, for his iron strength was ebbing. He dragged his burden down the bank and out on the ice.

The wind had risen but he headed instinctively in the direction he had followed the night before. Travelling was much slower now, with the powder snow and the cross wind and the mounting dizzy fatigue, but he laboured on. Dawn found him at the end of the chain of lakes, and he toiled up the bank and into a little grove.

The wind had swept and polished a bare space among the trees whose roots stood out like fingers from a hand. His feet slipped as he crossed it, but the clog slid smoothly after him until it caught beneath an exposed root. He was exhausted and barely conscious; at the sudden stop he plunged blindly into a big snowdrift. Suddenly the scent of man brought him quivering to his feet. He stared wildly about through the falling snow.

Not a hundred feet away was a cabin; the snow around it lay deep and untrodden but the scent of man was clear and unmistakable. It was an old scent, but it brought the collar of thick hair about his throat up to a bristle and narrowed his eyes and set his muscles tingling. He turned and plunged back toward the lake, and the loose end of the clog tightened under the next bare root.

He leaped in panic and the tightened chain threw him to the frozen ground. He crawled back, worn with the night's labour, and tested the roots with his teeth. They were weathered and tough, and both ends of the clog were pinned tight under them. He crept into the snowdrift and lay still. The snow fell softly and he closed his eyes in the sleep of complete exhaustion.

2. A DOG IS FREED

THE young wolf woke suddenly to a strange new sound. The snow had stopped and the sun was high. A hoarse drone like dim thunder came from the sky. Far above the trees a little silver plane circled the lake once and then dipped over the cabin.

The wolf shrank into the snowdrift with a growl as the shadow of a wing touched him. The plane climbed again and continued on its course into the east.

In the cabin of the twin-motored little transport, Don Murray wriggled restlessly in his seat. "Did you see it, Dad? Did you see the cabin?" he demanded.

His father was quietly stuffing papers into his brief case. "I certainly did," he said with a smile. "And I wasn't a bit surprised. It's been there for a long time, twelve years that I know of."

"Do you think I can ski out there to-night?" asked Don.

"You better get a good sleep at the mine first. You'll have to get your supplies together and check over your equipment. You know you'll have four days there anyway."

Don stared down at the snow-covered country. All winter he had been looking forward to the spring holiday and this trip.

Spring holiday! He smiled at the thought; it didn't look much like April in this country. Back home the newspapers were full of the opening of the baseball season; the snow had been gone for weeks and the fields were green and pleasant. Taking this trip to Canada was like moving the calendar back a month or more.

"Better fasten your belts!" called the pilot over his shoulder. "There's the landing strip under the right wing."

The little plane circled the mining camp—rounded Quonset huts, winterized tents, a couple of old log bunkhouses—and settled lightly to the cleared landing strip. Snow whirled up behind them as the pilot alternately gunned and idled the motors. They taxied up to a big man in boots and cape who was waiting for them.

"Have a good trip, Mr. Murray?" he greeted them. "You're right on time. Come on over to the mess hall and have something to eat."

Over steaming plates of stew Don explained his plans for the week to Mr. McLaren, the mine manager. "While Dad's busy here, I'll ski out there and open up the cabin. I've always wanted to see what the lake looked like with ice and snow on it. I'll just explore and loaf around there until the end of the week and then come back to fly home with Dad."

The big man rubbed his chin in thought. "Well, son, if you don't mind a few suggestions, I'd like to change your plans a little. First, the skis; they're not much use in the woods, and they'll be worse when this snow starts to thaw and thin out. Then your pack; you can't carry much of a load on skis. You say you want to travel light, but how's your appetite?"

The cook leaned on the end of the table. "Yes, that bacon and beans stuff is all right for an old-timer," he said, "but I've seen you eat before."

Don blushed as he looked down at his empty plate, and his father laughed.

"I think you ought to go on snowshoes—we've got them here in the supply room," Mr. McLaren went on with a smile. "Then we can let you have a couple of steaks, maybe a dozen eggs, some fresh bread . . ." he paused and glanced knowingly at the cook.

"I guess you're right!" agreed Don hastily, digging into the bowl of stew for a second helping.

He slept like a log that night under four blankets, and early the next morning he ate a breakfast that astonished even himself. He decided then to add some pancake flour and a bottle of maple syrup to his supplies.

"Got enough matches?" asked his father. "It'll take twenty-four hours to warm that place up."

"Don't trust that lake ice, and keep away from any bears you see," warned Mr. McLaren.

Don eased the pack higher on his shoulders and shuffled off on his snowshoes through the tall snow-covered evergreens. It was only eight miles to the camp and he ought to get there before noon.

It was warm travelling, although the snow was still crisp and dry underfoot. He opened his cape and tucked his heavy gloves under the shoulder straps of his pack to ease the weight. He still felt warm and tugged off his stocking cap to carry it in his hand.

After a mile or so he sat down in the shade of a huge fir to rest, and he was surprised at how fast he cooled off. In a couple of minutes he was glad to move out into the sun again. The contrast surprised him and he smiled to think how easily he might get sunburned while travelling on snowshoes.

It took him a minute or two to locate the trail again. It was amazing how much the snow changed the look of the country. He had tramped over this path half a dozen times every summer for nearly ten years, and still he had to watch carefully for familiar landmarks made strange by the snow. Several times he was forced to search for old tree blazes to make sure of his direction. The streams were snowed in, and he had to listen carefully for the hushed gurgle and clink that told him they were still flowing slowly under the heavy white blanket.

When he topped the last ridge and saw the lake

stretching smooth and white beyond the trees, he paused and took a long look around. There was no mistaking the spot where he had spent the summers almost as long as he could remember. He ploughed on through familiar trees to the snowed-in cabin.

He took off his snowshoes and used one as a rude shovel to clear the door. Inside it was musty and strangely quiet. He opened the shuttered windows to air the place and built fires in the stove and in the fireplace to drive out the long winter's chill. He also dug out the big can of kerosene and lighted all three burners of the oilstove for quicker warmth.

As he unloaded his pack, he suddenly realized how hungry he was. He stopped everything and fried up three eggs with bacon. That would hit the spot. McLaren knew what he was talking about when he insisted that he take a dozen and a half eggs.

The food restored his energy and he started out for a look at the lake. If it was still frozen firm, he might get in some fishing through the ice. It was open season for brown trout already, and there were always pan fish to be had. He slammed the cabin door behind him and swung down toward the lake with the axe over his shoulder.

Then he saw the grey yearling.

For an hour the young wolf had been alert and trembling. Now at the end of his chain he propped himself on his feeble forelegs and tried to snarl. He narrowed his eyes and lifted his lip, but his legs weakened beneath him and he slid back to the ground, half conscious.

A police dog, thought Don, a fine German Shepherd away up here! Then he saw the trap. What a shame! He rushed forward. The wolf made a final effort to gather his feet under him, but he could barely raise his head.

Don paused a few feet away. Let's see, now. Before helping any injured animal you had to muzzle it. He whipped out his bandanna handkerchief and took a half hitch in it. He knelt beside the wolf and eased the loop carefully over his nose. The yearling shook his head feebly and the long fur at the back of his neck rose, but in a moment the gag was secured.

Don turned his attention to the trap; it was a smooth-jawed double-spring Number Two. He took some slack in the chain, stepped on both springs, and eased the axe handle between the loosened jaws. The wolf's captured leg slid free.

His feet stirred and twitched, but Don picked him up in his arms and carried him into the cabin. Laying him on the rug before the open fire, he felt the injured leg carefully. It didn't seem to be broken. Probably the dog was suffering from hunger and thirst more than anything else.

Food and water would be easy. He scooped up a pail of snow at the door and set it on the stove. The steaks lay on the table, and he trimmed off the tail of one with lots of fat.

Maybe a stimulant would be a good idea first. Dad always had a bottle of some kind of liquor in the medicine chest. For pneumonia, he always said—or snake bite, although that was a joke.

Don brought out the bottle and poured a few table-spoonfuls into a pitcher. He took down a little funnel from over the sink and eased the handkerchief muzzle loose. That was how you gave medicine to a horse and it ought to work with a dog. Lifting the side of the upper lip cautiously, he slid the end of the funnel in beside the big grinding teeth and poured down the fiery liquor.

The wolf's throat gulped and he shivered all over. Can't blame him, thought Don, but the stuff ought to wake him up.

He poured a pie plate full of water and set it down in front of the animal; then he placed the meat on the floor beside it, slipped the muzzle off, and stepped back a few feet.

The yearling opened his eyes and struggled to sit up. He couldn't quite make it, but he sprawled over on his belly and thrust his nose into the water, gulping greedily. He straightened up a little and sniffed the meat; he pushed it for a moment with his nose, then lifted his lip and took it in his teeth. He threw back his head. Gone!

Don blinked at the lightning disappearance of the meat, and then went to the table for more. He could always eat beans himself, he thought with a momentary regret.

Bit by bit, he fed the rest of the steak to the starving

animal. It disappeared with alarming speed, but he showed
no ill effects.

When Don reached to pat the silvery-grey head, he
was surprised by the ghost of a growl which trembled
deep in the throat and an unconscious bristling of the
thick ruff. The poor dog is probably scared half to death,
he thought, as he drew back his hand and murmured
reassuring words. When he rose to tend the fires and
turn off the kerosene stove, the wolf struggled up on
three legs and tottered around experimentally.

Don watched him and wondered how he happened to
be out here in this lonely snowbound place. He must
have a home somewhere and an owner and a name. A
name! he thought. Lance would be a fitting name for
him. He was so lean and efficient looking, even in his
weakness. And his pointed muzzle and keen, direct eyes
carried out the idea, too.

"Lie down, Lance!" he ordered. "I'm going fishing."
He dug his drop line out of a drawer, picked up some
scraps of meat for bait, and opened the door.

Like a shot, the wolf slipped past him and limped away
into the snow.

"Here, Lance! Come here!" ordered the boy.

Lance was not interested. He circled clumsily away on
trembling legs.

Don picked up the axe and tramped down to the lake,
noticing that the dog watched for a moment and then
followed at a steady hundred-foot distance.

The ice alongshore was dry and solid, and Don walked out farther without any worries. A place with snow on it was best, he had heard, because the fish were not frightened by seeing your shadow through the ice.

Under the heavy crust the snow was dry and powdery, and he dug through to green ice in a couple of minutes. Then he took up the axe. A quarter of an hour later he decided the ice was thick enough to bear a trailer truck. He was all of ten inches down before he reached the water.

Lance limped a little closer as Don baited a hook and dropped it in. The bob floated sluggishly in the little hole, and it was almost impossible to see down into the dark water. Don remembered that out in the West they fished from shanties built on the ice and could watch the fish around their bait. The dark shanty was the trick. Maybe he could hood himself with his cape and see down into the water.

He unbuttoned the jacket and got down with his face close to the hole in the ice. Suddenly the bob jiggled and disappeared under the water. He grabbed the line and pulled experimentally. There was the steady throbbing tug that he remembered so well. Hand over hand he hauled up the catch, keeping the line well away from the sharp edges of ice.

It was a big perch that would run a good three quarters of a pound. He looked up at the sound of Lance's muffled whine and saw him edging closer in spite of himself.

Don loosened the hook and tossed the fish toward him. "Look it over, Lance! That's my breakfast for tomorrow."

The wolf scooped up the wriggling fish on the bounce and limped away with it between his teeth. A safe distance off, he sat down, shifted it deftly in his jaws until the head pointed down his throat, then chewed twice and swallowed. The fish was gone! Lance ran out his tongue and licked his muzzle.

"Whew!" whistled Don. "It looks as though you've done that before, Lance." Maybe he was an Eskimo's dog. They were fed on fish, but Don remembered it was dried fish. And this was a long way from home for an Eskimo's dog.

He baited the hook and dropped it in again. This time he took off his cape and masked the hole with it, sprawling face down and putting his head under it. He could see clearly now. The bait was surrounded by a little circle of fish, just as he had often seen it in the clear shallows of summertime.

A big fellow darted from the shadows of a withered weed bed twenty feet away. He charged in like a finny torpedo, and the smaller fish scattered as he grabbed the bait.

Don jerked the line to set the hook, and sent his cape flying as he sat up. The line was really heavy this time, and both his hands were wrist-deep in icy water keeping it away from the sharp edges of the hole.

He was glad it was a strong line and a short haul. If the trout had been able to do some real running, it might have been able to snap it. Hand over hand he hauled the fish up and flipped it out on the ice. It was a good three pounds. Lance whimpered hungrily.

"This one is for me!" announced Don. "You get the next one."

He moved the bob a little farther up on the line. If his bait lay deeper he might lure some more big fellows out of the shadows. He spread the cape and stuck his head under to drop his line. It was only a couple of minutes before a sizable perch hooked himself.

As Don threw back his coat and sat up, there was a hasty scratching of paws at his side, and a furry tail brushed his arm. He looked up to see Lance hobbling off with the big trout in his mouth. A hundred feet away he sat down and made four huge bites of it.

Don was almost too surprised to haul up the perch. "Gosh, you must be hungry, boy!" He took the perch off the hook and started to roll up his line. "And so am I!"

Lance nosed the spot where the trout had been a moment before. Then he sat back and sniffed the air.

"Do you want this one too?" asked Don, holding up the big perch.

Lance licked his chops. Don tossed it to him and it vanished as quickly as the first.

"Maybe I ought to catch you another one," Don said

B

thoughtfully. "But you must be pretty near full. That's four or five pounds of fish on top of a pound or more of steak. I think that's enough for to-day. You haven't eaten for a long time. Better go slow." He shook the snow out of his cape and put it on. "I haven't eaten for a long time myself, come to think of it. I'm about ready for that other steak," he said, as he slung the axe over his shoulder. "This is the first time I've ever come back empty-handed from fishing out here."

The sun was down behind the snow-covered hills across the ice and chilly gusts swept through the trees. Fine snow was sifting from the loaded branches and riding the wind.

Don hurried into the cabin, leaving the door open behind him. He loaded the stove and the fireplace with wood and went out again to call Lance, who had kept his distance from the cabin.

"Here, boy! It's nice and warm in here."

The grey wolf walked a bit farther away and lay down in the snow. Don coaxed vainly for several minutes and then his hunger called him back to the stove and the steak.

Lance watched with erect ears while light showed at the windows and the alluring scents of cooking reached his nose. After a long time the door opened and Don called again. The wolf got stiffly to his feet but moved no nearer. Finally the boy set down a pie plate full of supper scraps and closed the door again.

Lance limped slowly to the pan and gulped down its contents. He ate a mouthful of snow and sniffed at the closed door before retreating to a safe bed in a snowbank. Later there came the clanking of wood into a stove, and the light went out. The wolf got to his feet and scouted carefully around the cabin. He paused on his way to nose at the empty trap. He scratched a hole in the snow, pushed the trap in and scrabbled snow loosely over it.

He went back to the door to sniff again before he limped off to his cold bed. It was a long time before he slept, and even then his ears lifted at every sound of moaning owl or rising wind or coals falling in the stove inside the cabin.

3. "AN AWFUL SMART DOG!"

DON was awake early the next morning, but Lance was up before him. He sprawled in the snow with erect ears, watching the door alertly. He listened to the banging of pans and wrinkled his nose at the scent of cooking.

After breakfast Don came out for the pie plate and loaded it with the remnants of breakfast—bits of bacon, a whole fried egg, two buckwheat cakes, and the bacon drippings from the frying pan.

Lance eyed the plate longingly, but still he backed away on three legs as Don advanced. Finally the boy understood and set the pan down on the ground.

The young wolf stayed where he was until Don retreated to the door. Then he walked up to the plate and gulped down its contents.

Don fixed the fires, donned his cape, and picked up his .22 rifle. He sat down on the doorstep to put on his snowshoes, and then set off along the lake shore, following the snowed-in line of a familiar path. Soon he realized that Lance was coming along behind him and he seemed to be moving more easily. Sometimes he ran on all four legs for a step or two, and he coursed back and forth across the path as any curious dog would do.

A quarter of a mile down the path they entered a grove of red pines, huge towering trees like the pillars of a stately building. Suddenly Lance flashed forward like a grey streak, and a red squirrel fled up a tree with a scolding stream of chatter. Twenty feet up he paused to stammer his rage at his narrow escape.

"I'll fix that fellow; he can't talk to us that way!" said Don, as he cocked his rifle. "We ought to clean them out anyway so the grey squirrels can have a chance." He sighted and carefully squeezed off a shot.

At the crack of the rifle the red squirrel dropped to the snowy ground and Lance whirled and disappeared like a grey shadow.

Don walked over and picked up his game. "Here, boy! Breakfast is ready," he called, and looked around.

He seemed to be alone in the grove. Then Lance cautiously stuck his head around the side of a big trunk.

"Come and get it or I'll throw it away," urged Don.

The wolf started forward, hesitated, and slunk back again.

"Little gun-shy, aren't you?" said Don. "That's no way to act. Here!"

He tossed the squirrel toward the foot of the tree. Lance sniffed once and came charging out like a whirlwind. He worried the little red animal for a moment and then gobbled it down.

He licked his chops and trotted nearer to Don. His fear of gunshots had wilted rapidly at the sight of food. He sat back with alert ears and watched the boy.

Suddenly he raced forward a hundred feet and scouted back and forth with his nose to the ground. Don followed and found himself falling farther and farther behind.

When the distance between them had lengthened to nearly two hundred feet, the wolf stopped dead in his tracks. He froze for a full minute and then began to creep forward in a half crouch. Slowly, with frequent pauses when he looked like a silvery statue, he slipped forward. He crouched lower and lower, weaving in and out among the trunks to keep a tree between him and his unseen quarry.

Finally with a sudden spatter of feet, he rushed. There was a short scuffle in the snow and a quick snarl from the wolf. Then he trotted back toward Don with the limp body of another red squirrel in his jaws.

"Looks as though you can get along without a rifle," said Don in surprise.

They went on through the grove and out into the brush. Don decided to try the experiment of curing Lance of his gun-shyness. The animal sat expectantly in the snow while the boy showed him the gun, and watched with interest as Don carefully aimed at a clump of cones on a lone pine.

Lance flinched slightly at the report and then dashed hopefully forward to examine the fallen cones. He seemed disappointed at finding nothing to eat and Don thought he saw a look of reproach in his eyes.

During the next half hour he became hardened to the shooting and showed no fear. He never failed, though, to stare hopefully forward after each shot and he always trotted up to examine any twigs or snow that fell from Don's targets.

The sun was high now and Don was beginning to feel the pangs of hunger. He took a short cut back to the cabin across the lake ice, with Lance galloping on ahead. He showed less and less of the limp and sometimes trotted along for several minutes on all four legs. The boy marvelled at the animal's vitality, which had brought him out of complete exhaustion in twenty-four hours. There was still a line across the trapped leg where the hair had been worn thin, but in every other way he was bubbling with life and vigour.

Don had no idea of the strength of the wolf blood and the centuries of selective breeding behind it. Through uncounted generations of cold and starvation and bitter struggles the weak had died off and the strong had lived to pass on their strength and intelligence to their cubs.

He hurried up to the cabin and grapped a hasty lunch of bread and jam and cocoa. It seemed a shame to stay indoors and cook while the sun was shining and the wind was crisp and clear across the stainless snow.

When he came out, Lance was sitting halfway down the path to the lake, trembling with impatience.

"I've got a new idea, boy," confided Don, while the wolf sat with his head held sideways and seemed to listen attentively. "I'm going to cut three or four holes and put tip-ups on them. Maybe I can catch enough fish to fill you up—and have a few left over for myself."

There were poles in the shed which held the firewood, and it took Don only a few minutes to trim and notch them for tell-tales. He bound four sets hastily together with wire and started for the lake. It was quite a load. The wolf leaped away nervously and retreated into the grove at the boy's approach. Don trudged on toward the lake and when he looked back, Lance was trotting along behind him at a safe distance. His tail flaunted happily from side to side and as soon as they reached the lake, he circled on ahead and led the way to yesterday's fishing place.

The hole had frozen over lightly but it was only a few minutes' work to clear it, fasten a baited line to the tip-up, and drop it in. Don moved off another thirty feet and began to chop a second hole where he had seen the shadowy remains of the weed bed the day before. Twice during the chopping he had to stop his work and take a perch from the drop line. They both disappeared like magic down Lance's eager throat.

When the second hole was opened, he set another tip-up and started on a third hole. It was hard going and he was sweating freely when he heard an eager whine from the wolf.

"Just a minute, Lance!" he called impatiently. "I'm pretty busy right here."

The wolf whined again and then—for the first time in his life—gave a weird series of barks, like a quavering howl broken down into shorter sounds. Don looked up, surprised by the strange sounds. The tip-ups at both holes were sticking straight up into the air, and the one at the second hole was swivelling wildly around.

A trout! he thought, and sprang for it. A trout it was, a fine two-pound beauty, but he saw no more of it after he took it from the hook, dropped it on the ice, and hurried to the other hole. By the time he had hauled up a half-pound bream, the trout had disappeared and Lance was licking his chops.

"You must have hollow legs, boy, but I'll fill them up to-day!" Don said as he tossed over his newest catch.

He managed to finish the third hole and set the line without any interruption, but then the fish started biting again. In half an hour he had a triangular path worn back and forth from line to line. He got only one more trout, but perch and bream were taking the bait freely and it was a lot of fun hauling them up. Lance lost some of his shyness in the heat of the game; he dashed happily from hole to hole as the signals tipped. Twice Don had to wave a hand at him to chase him away from the hole while he took the fish off the hook.

It was somewhere between the twelfth and fifteenth fish that the wolf began to show signs of losing his appetite. He stopped gulping them down whole and began to clamp them to the ice with his paws while he daintily bit out the tastier pieces.

Don went on fishing until he had half a dozen more, and then he pulled up and coiled the lines. He strung his catch and tramped back to camp, with the wolf padding slowly along some distance behind him.

He stoked up the fires and came out again to clean the fish. Lance was curled up half asleep in a nest he had scratched in a snowdrift. He took a vague interest in the fish cleaning and when it was done he came slowly over to inspect the refuse. Daintily he picked out several roes which Don had discarded, then ambled lazily back to his snowdrift.

Don fried the filleted fish with bacon and stuffed himself on the firm white morsels. He finished before sunset and came out with the scraps for Lance. It seemed so pleasant outdoors that he poured himself another huge cup of tea with condensed milk and sat on the doorstep to drink it.

The wind was from the south and carried a pleasant soft smell of thawing. Here and there through the grove was a faint tinkling drip of melting snow.

Lance finished the scraps very slowly and pushed the tin plate noisily around for several minutes as he licked it with his tongue. The salt of the bacon held the same lure for him that it does for all wild creatures and he lapped up every last grain. Then he strolled over without any urging and sprawled a few yards from Don's feet, his head resting on his outstretched forepaws. He closed his eyes and sighed deeply. Don thought at first that he was asleep, but then he saw that his ears were still erect and turned alertly to every sound—the unexpected drop of a clod of snow, the creaking of a laden branch in the soft wind, the crack of a pine knot in the stove.

At last his ears drooped slightly forward and his breathing slowed. Don rose silently and leaned forward to stroke his head lightly. Like an automatic mechanism his ruff bristled at the touch and he slipped from under the hand, lips writhing back to show his teeth in sudden fierceness. It was gone in a moment. He swung his tail and the bristled hair smoothed down. He sprawled on the ground once more, a little farther away.

Don did not try to touch him again. He sat and wondered about his history while the sun settled beyond the jagged skyline across the lake, and the wind took on the chill of the snow it blew across. He must be a thoroughbred, Don thought, judging by his appearance and his fierce independence. He must have been mistreated, too, or he would not be so frightened and jumpy. Perhaps he had run away from a cruel owner—

but there were no settlements for hundreds of miles to the south and none at all northward.

He might have survived an aeroplane crash. He might have been lost by a party of hunters or fishermen. Don thought of half a dozen possibilities but none of them seemed very probable. Finally the chill of the wind forced him to his feet. He stretched his stiffened arms and yawned. Lance got slowly to his feet and stretched himself, too, fore and aft like a cat.

Don stepped inside the door and lighted a lamp; then he came back. "Come on in, boy!" he coaxed. "It'll be pretty cold before morning."

Lance swung his tail sleepily and trotted off across the clearing to his bed in the snowbank. He curled up and thumped his tail several times before he settled down.

Back in the cabin Don piled up the logs in the fireplace and sat for a long time staring into the flames. How could he get his independent new pet back home with him? His first thought was of a collar and chain, but he dropped the idea almost at once. Lance was heavy and strong and he would set up a terrific fuss if he were forced to do anything he didn't want to do. If he went he would have to go willingly, at least as far as the mine. There he might be lured into a crate and shipped home. Once he was back in the States he could probably be tamed much more quickly.

Don went sleepily to bed and dreamed of displaying his new pet to admiring friends at home.

He was up early the next morning and ate breakfast

with a touch of sadness at the realization that his vacation was half gone. But the thought of Lance waiting outside cheered him. He opened the door and the young wolf leaped to his feet and stared at him before prancing skittishly away. Then he walked slowly back.

Don left the cabin door open to the morning sunlight while he did the dishes and packed material for a lunch on the trail. Lance came to the door several times to watch him. Once he whined persuasively, but he firmly refused to be lured indoors.

When Don strapped on his light pack, Lance waited until the boy donned his snowshoes and then he led the way on a long circuit around the lake. Don was delighted with his companion's skill on the long tramp. In the past he had learned that hiking through the woods with a dog was apt to be rather dull, because the animal's barking and his noisy trampling frightened every wild thing long before he came into sight.

It was different with Lance. He could slip through the brush like a fox, and he could creep up on a watchful squirrel or a chipmunk with all the silence and caution of a cat. He was not hungry this morning and he hunted for the fun of it. Once he froze into a point like a trained bird dog, and Don halted to watch him work. It was several minutes before the boy saw the quarry, but finally a stir against the snow revealed a big grey squirrel busily digging in a cleared space for some long-buried nut or pine cone.

Lance stalked the clearing in a wide half circle until he got behind the nearest tree. He waited for a moment when the squirrel was turned away from the trunk and then he slipped out into the open and crept nearer. Twenty feet from him Lance gave a ferocious growl.

The squirrel did not pause to look but scurried for a tree. Lance burst into motion and leaped clean over the fleeing prey to cut him off. He landed so close that the squirrel almost ran into his open jaws as he spun around.

The squirrel changed direction and headed for another tree a full fifty feet away. Lance bounded up beside him in three strides and practically pushed him out of his course with an outstretched nose. Completely panic-stricken now, the squirrel dashed up a sapling barely five feet tall. Lance stood up on his hind legs, gripped a branch in his teeth, and shook the tiny tree violently back and forth. The squirrel clung to the topmost twigs with his tail flirting wildly back and forth to balance the dizzy swaying.

After a final shake Lance let go and trotted back toward Don. The squirrel behind him was too frightened to move; he clung to his branch with a muttered churring that seemed to give voice to his paralyzing fear.

Don laughed and slapped his knee delightedly. "Boy, if you could play soccer what a defence man you'd make!"

Half an hour later Lance's wood sense saved him and Don from a real danger. The wolf was scouting a hundred yards ahead with his nose to an interesting track, when he suddenly flung up his head and froze in mid-stride. He stood for only a moment and then turned to slip back toward the boy with silent speed. He stopped near him and crouched to the ground with watchful eyes on the snowy woods ahead. Don ducked behind a tree and sank to his heels. For a moment he neither saw nor heard anything. Then came a crackling of brush from the right; it came nearer, and a huge brown form loomed among the trees.

It was a bear, and a big one—four or five hundred pounds. Don did not move. Then he saw two tiny figures following the bear, and the reason for Lance's caution became clear. Just out of hibernation, the bear would be ill-tempered enough, but with two cubs to protect she would be the most dangerous animal abroad in the woods for a month or two.

The boy and the wolf crouched in hiding until the bear family had disappeared among the trees.

Then Don straightened up and shook himself. "Nice scouting, Lance! That big character in the fur coat can move faster than you can for a short-distance sprint. I'm glad we didn't stumble on the family unexpectedly."

Lance started back along the way they had come. Don followed him without hesitation. He realized that it was safer not to take any chances; his .22 was about as useful as an air gun against such a big foe.

A mile back along their trail, he stopped and took off

his web shoes. "How about some vitamins, Lance?" he suggested, and began to break up twigs from a fallen branch. With his belt axe he chopped some heavy pieces for a fire platform, and laid his campfire.

Lance circled curiously around and watched the proceedings with alert ears. When the flames began to crackle among the kindling, he pranced warily away. He sniffed the smoke and coughed at its pungence, but finally circled to windward and lay down at a safe distance to watch it.

The meal was chops and bacon, the last fresh meat Don had brought from the mine, washed down with a tin of tomato juice. Lance raised his nose to savour the scents of frying food and walked closer to beg for a taste.

"Chop bones are bad for dogs!" warned Don. "I don't think I ought to give you these."

But Lance whined so hungrily that the boy gave in. He tossed the bones to him one at a time, and marvelled at the efficient way the young wolf champed the food to powder in his strong grinding teeth.

When everything had disappeared and the frying pan had cooled, he let Lance lick out the bacon grease. He cleaned it to a polish.

They sat and rested after the meal, watching the fire until it turned to red embers. When Don had covered it with snow, he said, "Let's get along, Lance. We might have time for a little ice fishing before supper. I want to see if those hollow legs of yours are filled up yet."

Lance seemed to understand and for the second time he tried to answer by breaking a howl into a series of quavering barks.

They made good time back to the cabin but their haste was wasted. The fish did not seem to be biting. Don set out all the tip-ups, but only one attracted any fish and the total catch was three small perch. Lance ate them very politely with no gulping, and Don began to realize that he was not used to regular meals.

That night as Don was eating a supper of pancakes and fried eggs, he made a decision. Perhaps it would be better to start back to-morrow instead of waiting for the next day. It would probably take a little coaxing to get Lance into the crowded camp, and it would be good to allow him a day or so to get used to people there before trying to get him into a crate for the plane trip home.

He figured it out carefully. They would start right after breakfast and he wouldn't give Lance anything to eat. They should reach the mine just after dinner when there weren't too many people around to frighten him. The lure of food should make it easier to bring the hungry dog into strange surroundings. Don's father and Mr. McLaren would have some suggestions about calming him. They might even be able to entice him into a house. Don's thoughts came to a sudden halt; that was the biggest problem, getting him indoors. Lance had never set foot inside the cabin since the day he had been carried in semi-conscious.

Don cleaned up the last pancake. Maybe he could do something right away about bringing him under a roof. He opened the cabin door and called to Lance.

The wolf sat up from his couch in the snow and looked over questioningly.

"Come, boy! Supper's ready." Don rattled the pie plate.

Lance trotted willingly over to the open door.

"Fried eggs! Come on in!"

The animal did not stir from the doorstep.

Don went back to the kerosene stove and put the frying pan over the flame. As soon as he left the door, Lance confidently mounted the step and stood there, wrinkling his nose in pleasure at the scent of sizzling bacon fat.

Don cracked an egg into the pan and the cheerful hissing brought the wolf a couple of steps inside the door. But as soon as Don left the stove to move nearer the door, Lance backed calmly out into the open.

Don cracked a second egg into the pan and again the wolf approached, this time a little nearer. Another move toward the door and he retraced his footsteps with no sign of haste. Don sighed in desperation, and the wolf ran out his tongue in a grin. He seemed to think it was some sort of game.

Finally Don gave up and fried the two eggs with no attempt to trap his pet. Before the eggs were finished, Lance was standing at his side, sniffing in appreciation.

Don turned the eggs out on the pie plate and blew on them to cool them. A burned nose would give Lance a poor opinion of houses at the very start. He put the plate on the floor and sat down beside the stove to watch the wolf eat. He was much more dainty now that his first fierce hunger had been eased.

Halfway through Lance's meal, Don rubbed his hands together. "Isn't it cold in here? I think I'll close the door."

He got up and strolled slowly toward it. Lance kept one eye on him, eating daintily all the while. Before he reached the door knob, there was a smooth unhurried patter of feet and the wolf was outside the door.

"I give up, boy. Finish your supper." Don slouched back to his chair in discouragement. When he got there, Lance was already back at his uncompleted dinner. He finished the eggs, then raised his head and sniffed politely at the frying pan.

The boy was deep in thought and paid no attention. Lance whined a soft question, looking at the boy and then up at the pan.

"I'm sorry, Lance. I wasn't paying attention." Don handed down the greasy pan. The wolf licked it clean and pushed it around noisily until the last bit of flavour had been extracted. Then he sat back and carefully licked his chops. He got to his feet and stared around the room curiously, but made no effort to approach anything. His eyes and ears and his lifted quivering nose told him all he wanted to know. Wagging his tail slowly, he padded

out of the door and across the clearing to his snow-
bank.

Don got up and closed the door behind him. He shook
his head in discouragement. "That's an awful smart dog,"
he muttered. "Smarter than me!"

4. LANCE RUNS AWAY

DON was up early the next morning and after breakfast he packed his kit. There was not much to carry back, because he could leave most of his stuff for use during the summer. He put up the shutters, doused the fires, and covered the chimneys. Squirrels could do a lot of damage if they got inside and started chewing things up.

Lance was interested in all the work and trailed around outside the house, watching everything he did. When Don finally closed the door and set off eastward toward the mine, the wolf dashed on ahead of him with waving tail.

It was the warmest day so far and the snow was soft and thinning. Here and there wide patches of open muddy ground showed on the south slopes and every stream tinkled and gurgled with snow water. On sheltered banks there were opening clusters of little white bloodroot flowers among the snow, and Don blinked in

amazement at a single purple butterfly in the sunlight.
There were more birds about, too. Inquisitive chickadees
followed Don and Lance, and jays squawked angrily as
the wolf slipped through the trees where they had already
built their nests.

Don stopped in astonishment at the sound of barking
dogs. It was not until Lance sat down and stared upward
that he realized it was the honking of a flight of wild
geese. He sighted the ragged wedge as it wavered northward high above him.

They travelled slowly because of the snow and because
Don did not want to arrive until after dinner. The wind
had backed around to the east and long before they got
to the camp, its sounds and scents would be reaching them.

They were still more than three miles away when
Lance began to show signs of uneasiness. He no longer
galloped ahead, nosing out game trails. He padded along
ten feet from the boy's side or followed suspiciously
behind him.

Once, when the wind brought the blast of a whistle,
the wolf sat down in the snow and refused to follow
Don. But coaxing and talking had a temporary effect.
Once more Lance followed reluctantly, slinking along
behind Don, with head and tail lowered, his watchful
eyes glancing from side to side among the trees.

With only a mile to go, the sound and scent of the big
camp became too much for the wolf. He sat down again
and paid no attention to jokes or cajoling. When Don

tried to pat him, he snarled and circled warily away. The sound of aeroplane motors was the last straw. A big DC-3 from the mine had taken off into the wind, made a circling turn, and headed west. It came down-wind directly toward them at about a thousand feet with its motors labouring for more altitude.

Lance shivered and crouched low at the growing roar. The shadow of the plane topped a little rise a half mile ahead and came scudding toward them down the snowy slope. The wolf turned tail and fled into the woods, covering the ground in great twenty-foot leaps. Don dropped his pack and shuffled desperately after him on the clumsy snowshoes. He tramped back for more than a mile without a glimpse of the sleek grey form. The tracks were clear in the snow, and twice there were places where Lance had stopped and turned to watch the boy approach. But he was gone.

Don sat down in the snow, completely discouraged. He could go back to the cabin on the lake, but he would not reach there before late afternoon. The plane was to leave the following afternoon. That would not leave much time to win back the animal's confidence and lead him again over the route to the mine. There seemed to be nothing he could do. It would be more than two months before he came back again for the summer vacation. A lot of things could happen in that time. Lance might wander away, someone else might find him, he might starve to death.

No, Don decided on second thought, he wouldn't starve. Not while he was able to hunt squirrels the way he did. But he might roam pretty far away in search of game and never find his way back to the cabin. It would be empty for weeks and Lance could easily forget about their friendship.

Two miles away the grey wolf was trotting steadily along the trail back to the cabin by the frozen lake. Although he knew the boy would not be there, something seemed to draw him to the place. It was not merely the knowledge that he had been helped and fed there; it was the feeling of friendship he had experienced—a new and strange feeling in his wild and wandering life.

His steady, tireless lope ate up the miles and he was back at the cabin by mid-afternoon. He searched carefully to make sure that no one had been there since he left. He tracked the boy's scent around the cabin and out upon the lake and back. He whined mournfully several times before finally curling up in his nest in the snow-bank. He was uneasy there and shifted to another bank of snow that was more sheltered from the wind. Long before sunset he was asleep. All through the winter he had slept by day and hunted by night, and now that the boy was gone he returned at once to his natural schedule.

When the late moon rose in the clouded east, he woke and stretched himself, sprawling in the snow. Then he rose and stretched more thoroughly and shook himself all over. He padded over and sniffed at the closed cabin door. He gave a low mournful whine, then sat back on his haunches and howled sadly at the yellow sliver of the waning moon.

All through the woods wild creatures shivered at the sound, although many of them had never heard a wolf howl before. Twice again Lance howled before starting on his silent hunt through the woods and frozen swamps.

At the mine Don was going over his story a second time for the benefit of Mr. McLaren, who had just come in.

"A police dog, you say?" asked the manager, as he tamped the bowl of his pipe and scratched a match along the back of his pants.

"A thoroughbred police dog!" said Don with some feeling. "I know something about dogs, and this one had all the points. He was a little heavy around the jaws and forequarters and he was thin around the ribs from not getting enough to eat. But with good feeding and grooming, I'd enter him in a show!"

Mr. McLaren puffed at his pipe for several minutes. "Did you ever see a wolf, son?" he asked finally.

Mr. Murray whistled in surprise and looked at his son with a new respect, but Don laughed and waved the idea away with a gesture. "Why, Mr. McLaren, I carried this fellow into the cabin and fed him with my own hands. I never patted him, but I think I could have."

The manager nodded. "Well, you know the Eskimos and the Alaskan Indians have tamed wolves—young ones, of course—and hitched them to their sledges with the dogs," he said at length. "And I've heard that over in Europe they breed German Shepherd dogs to the wolves —I think it's in Dalmatia—to develop dogs for police work. That's where the name police dog comes from."

Don was worried but he refused to admit it. They argued until bedtime without any agreement, and Don went to sleep still thinking of his lost pet. Dog or wolf, he was a fine animal. If he'd only had another week to tame him!

Back in the pinewoods, Lance was still hunting. He had caught only a couple of white-footed mice, but he was not really hungry and he prowled on through the woods more for pleasure than to find food. He was alert to everything that moved on the ground, in the trees, and in the air. He saw the huge white Arctic owl that drifted soundlessly through the air like sudden death, sighting everything that moved as well as he did. He knew that somewhere in the branches above him an ermine was prowling in search of quaking squirrels or sleeping birds.

In his night's prowl he reached a beaver dam ten miles away on a little stream that ran into the lake. He heard the faint bumping under the ice of the pond which told that the beaver were floating up the last of their winter supply of aspen logs. Anchored to the bottom by plasterings of mud, the store of bark provided their food through the frozen months.

At the farthest limit of his hunt Lance halted for a minute on top of a little ridge. Off to the north there were moose—a lot of them. He turned back without investigating further. At this time of the year they would still be in a yard—a wide stretch of woods where they had trampled down the snow. Even a starving wolf would be insane to venture into such a place. A single moose alone in deep snow, where his hoofs broke through at every step, would be fair game for a half-dozen alert wolves who could move lightly around on the frozen crust. But a herd of moose on good footing could destroy any lone wolf. Lance marked the location for future use; in a few weeks the big animals would begin to separate.

The moon was swinging lower in the west. He turned his back on it and loped homeward to the empty cabin. The east was glowing with the early light before the dawn when he bedded down in his snowdrift, tucked his nose under his curled tail, and went to sleep.

The next few weeks were busy and happy ones for Lance. The woods were stirring with life, and he scouted and ranged for miles in every direction except toward the mine. Every night he scoured the hills and valleys, and as the northern nights grew rapidly shorter he prowled and hunted during the daylight hours as well.

There was no shortage of food as the snow disappeared from the low places and southern slopes. Squirrels and chipmunks and nesting rabbits were soon so plentiful that he disdained the mice except for the fun of hunting them. Frogs croaked and boomed in the marshes and he took a puppy's delight in hunting them along the lake shore and the brooks. They tasted good, too. Sometimes he haunted the shallow ripples where trout and perch came to spawn in the water that ran low and clear over the pebbly bottom.

One dark night he slipped like a darker shadow up to his favourite fishing place and found a northward-ranging raccoon with a brood of kittens there. The black-masked mother was scooping out the fish with clever, almost human hands and tossing them up on the bank where her three tiny youngsters sat in a solemn row. When half a dozen silver perch were flopping among the grass, the wolf gave a deep growl and walked calmly forward. The raccoon flashed her teeth in a show of anger, but it was only a trick to let the kittens escape into the trees before she followed them like a streak.

Fifteen hundred miles to the south, Don Murray had received news of his friend.

Mr. Murray sat down at the supper table one night with an enigmatic smile on his face. "I got a letter from

McLaren to-day," he announced.

"That so?" said Don. "Did he say anything about that crazy idea of his?"

"He sent me a newspaper clipping," answered his father, hunting through a handful of papers extracted from his inside coat pocket. "Here it is."

Don picked it up with quickening interest. "Hey, this is in French!" he objected.

"Yes." His father laughed. "I know you took French for a year but I had our Canadian correspondent translate it for me." He handed over a typewritten sheet.

Don grabbed it eagerly.

A local reporter writes that J. Lalibert, trapper, visited his cousin Francois Lalibert at St. Jerome-de-Metabachouan last week after a winter in the woods. He reported a fine season and a good catch. Among his furs were two large wolfskins in fair condition. These are the first to be obtained in that area in many years. Lalibert shot the two wolves and reported that at least one escaped his rifle, only to be caught in one of his traps. The beast dragged the trap several miles, after which the trail was wiped out by a snowstorm. Local hunters are deeply interested.

"Well, what do you say now?" asked his father.

Don stared out of the window. The newspaper story confirmed his own secret belief, but he hated to admit it.

"I can't figure out how a police dog would be running with a pack of wolves," he said with a smile.

"I give up," said his father. "That sounds like proof to me."

"I'll never spend another peaceful night in that cabin," exclaimed his mother. "Hadn't we better take some dogs up with us in June?"

"We'll have a dog," announced Don stubbornly. "It'll be Lance. I'll bet he's still waiting up there for me." He voiced his hope confidently but his heart was not in it.

In the grove beside the cabin Lance was yawning and stretching after a long, warm afternoon of slumber. He walked slowly down to the bright lake and drank silently. Then he stood for a moment and stretched out his head to sniff the wind from the north-west.

In spite of the easy living which had filled him out in the last six weeks, he had hardened. His long runs over the hills and through the woods had put him in splendid condition, and every nerve and muscle tingled with life. He was a fine hunting machine, packed with energy and explosive with strength.

The wind brought him the scent of moose, and he stood for several minutes gathering all the news the breeze could give him. His head lifted slowly with each breath he took as he measured the distance and probable location of the huge creature. Lance weighed less than eighty pounds and the moose might run as heavy as half a ton, but the killer instinct outweighed everything else. Lance's nose told him that this was a cow moose, probably with a calf, and he set off in a swift, distance-eating stride to circle the lake and find her.

For five miles he loped along, guiding himself by the memory of the air-borne scent that had reached him across the lake. Then he picked up a direct scent on the slight breeze and he turned into the wind to follow it. Half a mile farther on he slowed to a trot and began casting back and forth, nose to the ground, to pick up the trail. His alert ears remained erect although he knew there would be almost no noise from the huge clumsy-looking animal. Despite her rangy bulk, she could slip through the underbrush as silently as he.

At last he struck the clear, unmistakable trail where the animal had passed with a young calf. The two had been browsing on green moss and young shoots. Lance trembled eagerly and increased his pace. He galloped forward with nose low to the ground and eyes straining forward under wrinkled brows. The trail became hotter and he slowed his pace again. There was a bare chance that he could slip up on the browsing animals. He slunk like a shadow through the trees in a half crouch. Not a leaf rustled, not a twig cracked as he drifted forward on the trail of the moose.

To surprise her, however, was almost impossible. The cow moose, with her great height and her eyes set sideways to see in two directions at once, glimpsed the grey figure in the distance. She leaped into flight on the instant, but her little calf was a handicap. She shambled into a trot, nosing the rickety little calf before her into a thicket of scrub oak.

Lance rocketed forward with a fierce hunting howl. The moose turned to face him as she backed into the shelter of the brush with her calf behind her, safe for the moment. The wolf drove forward as though to leap, and then checked his rush at the last instant as a great razor-edged hoof lashed out to strike him down. He circled the thicket while the moose backed deeper among the bushes which protected her from his swift dashes.

Lance paced restlessly around the patch of brush, looking the ground over and planning his attack. The moose circled warily around her calf, watching for any possible rush. There was one spot among the low under-growth where the bushes were sparse and thin. The wolf saw this was the key spot, but he circled twice around the thicket before stopping. Then he lay down in front of the opening as though to rest.

The moose faced him across that weak link in her defences, alert to his every move. Lance's eyes took in the location of every bush and branch while his keen brain shaped his moves. It would be fatal to be trapped among those tangled twigs where the moose could slash and stamp with all the fury of her nine hundred pounds of bone and muscle.

Suddenly he lunged forward as though to spring for the throat. At the last instant he crouched to the ground and watched the great hoof slash like an axe through the air. He retreated slowly with the limit of that stroke clearly pictured in his mind. That far he could go in

safety. He lolled on the ground for five minutes, while
the moose waited in anxious quiet and the calf cowered
against her.

Without warning he leaped forward again, and again
he crouched with head pressed to the ground while the
great hoof covered the same arc through the air and
landed on the same spot of ground. Then he walked back
to his vantage point, where he turned himself in a careful
circle as though to bed down for another few minutes'
rest. Instead, he launched himself suddenly forward in
another attack, flattening again on the ground just short
of the moose's kick. The great hoof struck out and as it
touched the ground, the crouching wolf gripped it by
the fetlock.

It was counter-attacking such as a skilled boxer might
have envied. Only for an instant did Lance keep the
punishing hold that slashed the skin and grazed the bone.
As soon as he felt the moose put her weight on the foot
he held, he knew the other great hoof was rising for a
stroke and he flung himself backward out of danger.
By half a yard he slipped clear. He drew back for a
moment, breathing deeply. The great animal's left foot
was not disabled, but she would be wary of another such
attack.

He did not attempt to disguise his next charge; he
crouched and balanced as he prepared for it. When he
finally rushed, the moose was prepared, too. Her hoofs
lashed out in a one-two, the left short and the right in

c

front of it where the wolf would be if he attempted the snap at her fetlock. Lance crouched, well clear of the blows, and photographed in his mind their limit and their timing. Now he was ready for the knockout. He crouched and stared at the injured foot, then drove forward for the kill.

Again the mòose lashed out, one-two, with both hooves. And then, in a split second, she realized too late that she had been tricked. Both her forefeet were on the ground, and the wolf was crouched to spring directly beneath her. It was the sort of second thought a boxer might have in the last instant before the knockout blow followed the perfect feint.

Lance flung himself straight upward at her throat and his teeth gripped like a steel trap. He hung with his full weight upon her neck for a moment; then he whipped his heavy body back and forth in a frenzy of energy as he felt the hot blood flood over his muzzle and the sobbing breath gurgle in the choking throat. The moose tried to lift a menacing hoof, but the weight dragged her down. She staggered a pace and went forward on her knees. With glazing eyes she rolled over and the wolf regained his feet to tear, growling, at her throat.

In a few minutes his hunting fury was spent and the bristling of his ruff relaxed. He sniffed curiously at the big animal he had killed, and when the trembling calf tottered out of the bushes, he growled automatically but allowed it to escape into the woods. He lay down beside his prey and for some time stared at it. Then he rose and began a leisurely meal.

While he ate, he growled and grumbled fiercely as his savage ancestors had done, although there were no enemies to be frightened away and no rival wolves to dispute his kill. When he had finished, he bedded down on the soft pine needles and slept. Throughout the entire hunt and the final battle he had been driven more by instinct than by hunger. It was a fine cool day, he had been feeling especially strong and vigorous, and there was big game to be scented. He had trailed and killed it. It was the same sort of thing that thousands of well-fed human hunters do every year.

When Lance awoke he sprang instantly to his feet with every nerve tingling. It was in the darkness before moonrise and something was stealing his food. He leaped forward, and an alert little fox fled like a ghost into the shadows.

Lance prowled around the carcass, grumbling deep in his throat, before making another hearty meal and going back to sleep. For two days he alternately ate and slept, rousing to drive away a half-grown black bear at one time and a spitting Canadian lynx at another. Finally he lost interest in the venison and wandered slowly back to the cabin across the lake.

5. DON COMES BACK

AS Lance came near the cabin he caught a strange scent, a mixture of man and smoke and iron that awoke all his suspicions. He circled widely around the camp and at one spot picked up the trail of two men. He scouted along it for a mile or more in the direction of the mine and then gave it up to return to the cabin.

He stalked in a wide circle around the area before venturing closer. The men had gone back to the mine from which they had come, he knew, but their scent lingered on strongly and he quivered with suspicion and unrest. When he finally approached the cabin, he walked with careful steps as though every patch of ground might explode into a trap. He investigated and sniffed at everything. Two men had been there; they had lived a while in the cabin and had built fires. They had caught fish in the lake.

What was most suspicious of all, they had changed

the appearance of the cabin. A huge shed behind it stood open and empty. Next to it was a tall fence of brush that enclosed a stretch of bare ground. Lance had never seen a garden and the seeded rows with their bright-coloured envelopes at each end were strange and frightening. Tin cans and bits of ribbon, strung to scare away birds, fluttered and tinkled in the wind from the lake. He stayed far away from the garden. Down at the bank of the lake a float had been bolted together and anchored six feet from shore. A heavy plank led out to it. Near it lay two canoes, bottom up.

Lance scouted around all the new things at a careful distance. He growled and grumbled suspiciously. Once he caught a faint and very old scent of the boy who had been there in the snow. He sniffed and whined, but it did not overcome his fear. He could not feel at ease after these changes in the camp. He retreated a quarter of a mile to the grove of red pines and slept there that day to the noisy discomfort of the squirrels who lived among the trees.

For several days he continued to visit the cabin and the grove around it, sniffing for traps and suspicious of everything. At length he lost interest and left the place for good. When he passed the camp on his goings and comings around the lake, he circled wide around it or sat for a while to look at it from a distance.

Then came a warm, sunny noon when he woke among the pines with a sudden feeling of uneasiness. He rose and stretched himself while the red squirrels fled into the treetops, scolding shrilly. Lance raised his head high and sniffed deeply to learn what had roused him. There was no breeze in the windless noon and he scented only the pines and the squirrels and a venturesome fox who had passed the day before. His ears turned inquiringly back and forth and suddenly he caught a strange mixture of sounds far in the distance. There were voices and thumping feet and an odd shrill bark that was too high-pitched to be a fox's. He trotted forth to investigate.

Halfway to camp he stopped. He caught the unmistakable scent of the boy who had saved him from the trap. He stopped breathing and stood like a statue to listen. Faint and far he heard a voice. Old memories moved and wakened.

"Here, Lance! Here, Lance!"

The wolf whined uneasily and padded back and forth on restless feet. Something urged him to go forward, but the strangeness of those other scents and noises warned him to caution. He trotted slowly toward the camp and cut back and forth across the trail to the mine, watching and listening.

Far off he saw a stir among the spruce branches and three figures came into view, humped with their big packs. One was the boy, all right, but the others were men and strangers. Behind them came another figure, a girl with a smaller pack, leading on a leash the tiny creature whose shrill bark had carried so far ahead of him. Lance turned and crept back into hiding among the brush. He watched the file approach.

"Here, Lance!" called the boy again, and the wolf's tail swung slowly back and forth.

"He isn't here!" said the girl. "Now can I turn Jitters loose?"

"If only you hadn't brought that darned mutt!" exclaimed Don. "Oh, go ahead, Judy, and let him run. I hope a chipmunk eats him up."

Judy stooped and unsnapped the leash. The tiny cocker spaniel set out like a black streak. He tore happily down the path and skidded suddenly to a stop as he crossed the fresh trail of Lance. He whined frantically at the scent and galloped wildly away to follow it in the wrong direction. In his hiding place, Lance sniffed his disdain and turned his attention to the rest of the party as they tramped on to the cabin.

Don looked downcast but his father and Mr. McLaren seemed a bit relieved.

"I think it's just as well we don't have to worry about Lance," said Mr. Murray. "He might have acted very well with you alone, but a crowd around might excite him. We could have had some real trouble."

"That's right!" Mr. McLaren laughed. "He might even have eaten up Jitters. Then think how you'd feel!"

Don grinned wickedly. "Oh, how terrible!" he said, in a shrill imitation of his younger sister's voice.

They unhooked their heavy packs and let them slip to the ground.

"How about a swim, son?" said Mr. Murray. "The last one in has to cook dinner!"

In five minutes the two men and the boy were in the water and Jitters was yelping his elation from the float. Lance slunk nearer in the underbrush to watch and whimper his excitement.

Suddenly a pair of bare feet dashed past his nose as he lay in the brush, and Judy's shrill voice called to Jitters. She never saw Lance, but he was startled and crept deeper into the scrub growth. Still he kept watch on the camp. When the four people trailed up the path, arguing happily over who should cook dinner, he saw them. He saw smoke curl from the chimney and he watched when they came out afterward to lounge in the sun before unpacking.

All through the long afternoon he lurked in hiding, learning to know everyone by sight and scent. Gradually he moved his hiding places farther and farther back, as the newcomers covered more ground in their travelling to and fro. He was both attracted and frightened by the bustle and the unaccustomed voices.

Not until the last light had been put out in the cabin, did he leave his shelter. Then he slipped like a ghost into the clearing and moved softly about, examining everything with eyes and nose. He felt no fear of traps this time but still he moved quietly because of some vague uneasiness that he could not understand.

For a week he spied on the clearing, and only Jitters

knew of his presence. The little cocker spaniel stumbled over him one day where he drowsed in a grassy glade, and rushed him in a shrieking fury. Lance side-stepped, circled the little dog's headlong attack, and fled with dignity into the shadows. He was out of sight in a few seconds, but for an hour Jitters ran up and down his trail in a loud frenzy.

After two days Mr. McLaren and Don returned to the mine. On the following day the boy came back and this time his mother accompanied him. Lance, who had trailed Don at a distance to within a mile of the mine, picked him up next morning on the return trip. Hidden in the pinewoods he watched Don and his mother all the way back to the cabin.

Lance got to know the routine of the camp as though he were one of the group. He was alert and watchful at the first stirring in the morning, when the sun shone bright and hot on the grove or loomed moonlike through the mists from the lake. He listened for the slap of the screen door as Don and his father went down to the lake for a dip before breakfast, and for the squeak of the pump that came later. He sniffed the appetizing aromas of bacon and pancakes and the strange reek of Mr. Murray's pipe, which always followed.

He knew to the minute the time when little Jitters would come dashing out of the cabin door like a black streak and race for the canoe float, where he would bark his fierce daily defiance at his echo from across the lake.

Judy would come out next and curl up in the hammock with a book or stroll through the woods after Jitters.

In mid-morning Don and his father would take the big canoe and paddle out to a favourite pickerel or bass bed around the lake. Lance always followed these expeditions from the shore, circling around swamp and inlet and never losing sight of the boy for more than a few minutes.

The fishermen usually returned for lunch and then, during the hot days at the end of June and the beginning of July, they spent the afternoon swimming in the chilly lake with intervals of lounging in the hot northern sun between dips. During these hours Lance would drowse and doze in the brush, although he was always careful to pick a spot down-wind from camp. He did not want little Jitters to come upon him again without warning.

One morning he had a real fright. A huge white pine towered eighty feet into the air at the edge of the cabin clearing, and Mr. Murray had often worried for fear a storm might bring it down upon the roof. He decided to chop it down and remove the threat for good.

He and Don took turns at hewing the undercut, making sure the tree would fall out into the brush, and then Don stopped for a swim while his father toiled on. Lance lay snugly among the undergrowth watching them. He had slipped away earlier at the sound of the first strokes of the axe and then crept back when nothing dangerous followed the unusual noise.

Gradually the monotonous strokes of the axe blended into the drowsy hum of crickets and the other sleepy sounds of the summer day. Lance watched Don as he dived and swam around the dock while Jitters danced back and forth or waded shoulder-deep into the cool water. He felt a great yearning to be closer to these people and their strange harmless little animal.

Suddenly a harsh crackling brought the prickling hair up on his back and set his muscles trembling with tension. He half rose to his feet and stared around.

"Timber!" called Mr. Murray triumphantly.

High overhead there was an ominous whistling in the air. The memory of his puppy days, when hawks and owls were a deadly threat, sent Lance scuttling to one side even as he looked up. The sight of the great tree whipping down at him out of the sky made his blood pound wildly and he leaped into flight as though a trigger had been pulled. He raced madly through the brush as the huge trunk crashed to the quaking earth. The snapping and crackling of limbs as it settled among the brush spurred him to wilder flight. He was a mile away before he slowed his pace and it was two days before he ventured so close to camp again. Always after that he viewed Mr. Murray with great respect and an admiring sort of fear.

The next night after supper Don lounged on the dock in the last sunlight with Jitters, staring into the water where tiny minnows and clumsy lizard-like newts glided slowly. Idly he raised his head and glanced across the lake. A sudden movement caught his eye on an open stretch of shore a quarter of a mile away. Something was moving slowly through the grass. Stirred by curiosity, he dropped into the small canoe, pushed the eager Jitters back on the dock, and paddled out into the lake. Aiming at the spot where he had seen the movement, he swept the little craft forward with easy strokes. Before he was halfway to his goal, a round clumsy turtle waddled out of the grass and plunged into the water.

Eggs, he thought, turtle eggs! He ran the canoe up on the shore at the very spot where the big creature had returned to the water. In the slanting light of the sun the trail was clearly marked through the crushed grass and he had no trouble in finding the spot where the turtle had deposited her batch of eggs. The ground was bare and the loose earth had been kicked carelessly back to fill the hole she had dug.

"That's a lazy way to raise a family," murmured Don as he brushed the earth gently away. A few inches down he came to the eggs. Almost round and half the size of hens' eggs, the shells were still soft to the touch. He dropped a couple into the pockets of his shirt and started to push earth back over the rest.

He stopped. "The heck with them!" he muttered. "Let the raccoons have them. The more turtles, the less fish!" He climbed into the canoe and paddled home to display his find.

Three hours later, when the last glow of the sunset had burned away, Lance came padding silently by on one of his lonely errands. At the well-known scent of the boy, he froze to a statue and sniffed the air for several minutes before he stole softly through the darkness to the open hole and the familiar footprints. He traced Don's path to the water's edge and back again. Then he scratched the eggs out on the ground and settled down with them between his outstretched forepaws. He ate slowly and delicately with a warm feeling that he had not known since those first half-forgotten days with the boy.

One scorching, breathless morning a few days later, Mr. Murray decided against the daily fishing trip. "That sun is too hot for me, Don!" he objected. "You take the little canoe and go alone. I'll stay home and pray for rain."

"I wish you'd come, Dad," insisted Don. "I was thinking of going down to that third lake to-day. We haven't fished it this year and the big fellows down there must be starving."

"Go ahead and feed them," said his father. "But you'd better take a lunch or you'll be starving yourself before you get back. That's a long trip."

Don piled his kit into the smaller canoe and ran it into the water while the family gathered to see him off.

"Now be careful, Donald!" urged his mother.

"Watch out for thunderstorms this afternoon," warned his father. "They can kick up some big waves in a hurry down there."

Don pushed off and dipped his paddle with a swing of his shoulders. This little canoe was a pleasure to drive along; it gurgled through the water with a hissing whisper of speed. He drove hard across the lake toward the gap among the trees that marked the passage into the lower lake. Once through it, he slowed down to look about him. He had not seen this place since the summer before. There was the brook where the beavers had been chopping down trees. The chewed stumps stood all around and a single trimmed tree trunk lay on the ground, but the beavers were nowhere in sight. Fearless hawks posed on the tops of dead trees and turtles drowsed in the sun on grounded logs.

Farther on, as he passed a shadowy little inlet among big trees, a bear crashed away through the brush at the sight of him. He had a tight, slightly nervous feeling and he wondered if pioneers felt like that. He always had the sensation when he was out on a strange lake.

The canoe was a light bubble on this unknown depth of water. A mile away on either side was firm earth, but out here it was almost like flying. He was suspended on the lake with the wide sky above him and sailing clouds reflected below him. He drove on with steady strokes toward the third lake. He paddled into it about noon, but he was too hungry to start fishing right away. He ran the canoe up on a little point of land between two huge rocks and went ashore to eat lunch.

Lance had followed him all the long ten-mile trip, but he had come along the opposite shore. He lay in a thicket and watched the boy as he built a little fire on a rock to keep the flies away while he ate. The lake water lapped and gurgled at the shore, and a formation of wild ducks circled nervously before settling into a swamp along the edge.

When Don had finished eating, he kicked the fire into the lake and pushed out again. At a promising spot, he stowed the paddle carefully and rigged his pole. It was a good location. The bass bit furiously and he had so much fun that he threw back all but the biggest. In an hour he had his limit; he glanced around for the sun to get an idea of the time.

Dad had been right. A huge thunderhead was piling up in towers in the west, and it was ten miles to home. He tucked his rod under the thwarts and hauled out the paddle with a sigh. It was always so much harder to paddle home. He drove hard, whipping the paddle from one side of the canoe to the other, careless of the trickle of water that ran down the handle. It was pleasant in the hot, sticky work to feel the cool drops on his arms. The passage into the second lake was just ahead when he looked back again.

The cloud had spread and flattened, with jagged lightning flashes playing in it, but it looked as though it

were going to pass behind him. He slid through the
narrow pass and saw how fast he was going by the trees
reeling by. He dipped his paddle with new vigour and
headed straight across the open water toward the home
lake. His palms were stinging and his shoulders and back
began to ache with the effort. Midway across the second
lake, the sun disappeared and he could see the huge cloud
shadow scudding ahead of him across the still water. He
stopped paddling to look back. The rain was going to
miss him all right; the storm was moving off to the eastward, trailing long curtains of rain that already blotted
out the third lake.

Then the wind struck.

One minute the lake was a gun-metal mirror in the
sudden shadow, and the next minute a million ripples
rose and climbed into choppy little waves. The canoe,
moving across the wind, lost speed and began to bob
nervously up and down. The wind swooped down in
heavy gusts and in a few minutes the waves had built up
to a foot in height. The canoe swerved out of its course
and Don fought it back into line with the opening to the
home lake. It wavered again and he had to head it halfway into the wind to make any forward progress at all.

The air was cold and he shivered despite the hard work.
At times the canoe yawed violently to one side in sudden
blusters of wind; once it skidded sideways as he dipped
for a stroke and caught the paddle under it. It rocked
violently before he could whip the paddle clear and take

a steadying stroke. In fifteen minutes of hard struggling he reached the pass between the two lakes, and the canoe slid into a hundred yards of calmer water. It rocked gently there where the trees shielded it from the wind, and Don rested his paddle across the gunwales and took a breather.

The home lake ahead looked fierce and choppy, and he thought for a moment of running the craft ashore and walking the rest of the way. But it would mean coming back later through the heavy brush, and he dropped the plan. Fifty yards away on shore, Lance watched from cover and whined softly.

Don drove onward into the mounting waves, fighting his way homeward. The wind seemed to be increasing, and he risked a look backward. The cloud was not passing; it seemed to have changed direction a little and spread nearer. Halfway to the landing he began to realize that he was almost exhausted. His arms were heavy and the paddle was like lead. The wind was stronger, too, and he wasn't making much progress against it.

He heard two shots faintly through the wind. Probably they had sighted him from the camp and were encouraging him. He peered ahead. His father stood on the canoe float; he was waving him in toward shore. The water must be rougher up ahead. He decided that he didn't need much persuading. He fought the bow around into the wind and drove for shore, half a mile away. The canoe rose easier now that it met the waves head on, rising and falling as they swept past, but the paddling was much harder. He dipped alternately to right and left, putting all his weight into every stroke. He could see the progress he was making. The trees loomed higher and higher, and he could glimpse a strip of smoother water close inshore. That was what his father meant; he could get home easily by hugging the bank.

Then it happened. The paddle was wet and slippery and his hands were tired. As he leaned into a stroke, the cramped fingers of his lower hand skidded on the smooth wood, the paddle slipped free, and the force of his shoulder swing drove it down and away. He grabbed for it as it slid backward through the water, and the canoe swayed drunkenly. He gripped the sides and balanced it with his body, but the bow had been caught in the wind and a wave slopped over the side. The bottom was an inch deep in water.

This was rough. A hundred feet to go, and with no paddle it might as well have been a mile. He tried paddling with his hands and made no progress at all. The canoe was drifting out fast. He would have to swim for it. He slipped off his moccasins and tied them to a thwart. Then he leaned forward and gripped the gunwales as he lifted himself carefully over the side. The canoe skidded as he pushed it away, and the ice-cold water closed over his head. He went down a long way before he kicked out and started to rise. One stockinged foot scraped rock as he thrust. It must be eight or ten feet deep here, he thought. He broke the surface and slung the water out of his face with a quick twist of his head.

The canoe floated bottom up a few yards away and he swam over to it. A groping thrust underneath told him that his rod was still there, but all the fish must have gone. He pulled himself along to the stern and tried to drive the canoe ahead of him by kicking his feet. It was slow work and he made very little progress. He kicked harder—flutter kick and frog kick—and still the wind seemed to be winning. He peered around the side at last and saw that he was actually gaining; the shore was only twenty-five feet away. He let himself down and one waving foot touched bottom. He would have to right the canoe some time and he might as well start now. He pulled himself around to one side, gripping the submerged gunwales, and bore down on it with all his weight. The craft rolled sluggishly back and forth in the water.

On shore Lance padded nervously out of the brush and stood watching him. Don was too busy to notice. He put all his strength into the job of rocking the canoe over. Twice it seemed on the point of turning over as he reached up and grabbed the slippery keel, and twice it swung back. At last he got a good grip on the keel and the craft began to swing slowly and clumsily on to its side. A sudden gust of wind caught the turning canoe and speeded its progress. Don's hand lost its hold at the sudden motion and he slipped back into the water.

He saw the keel slamming down on him and he ducked his head sideways, but the full force of the blow crashed against his temple. A bright light seemed to flare in his eyes for an instant and he struck out feebly with arms and legs. Then he went limp and began to sink slowly, face down in the water.

6. LANCE RETURNS A FAVOUR

AS Don sank into the water, Lance dashed to the edge of
the lake and whimpered nervously. He hesitated for only
a moment, prancing uncertainly back and forth, before
he leaped twice his length out into the water. He sank
to his nose and came up swimming strongly. He reached
the spot where Don had disappeared, and circled for a
moment, staring about him. Don drifted closer to the
surface, and the wolf seized a limp arm carefully in his
jaws and tugged the boy clumsily toward shore.

It was a hard struggle; Don's trailing legs dragged
against the wolf's threshing hind feet and slowed his
progress. Once the water closed over both their heads
and Lance nearly strangled, but he forced his head above
water and forged ahead. His great chest was sobbing
with effort when he felt the rocky bottom under his feet.
Painfully he dragged the boy halfway out on the bank
and then staggered ashore to shake the dripping water

from his coat. He returned to sniff anxiously at Don and drag him a few inches farther up on the land. Then he sat back on his haunches and howled mournfully at the clouds.

A few minutes later the big canoe rounded the point and Judy and Mr. Murray sighted the wolf on shore. He saw them at the same instant and leaped nervously back into the brush. He stopped and hesitated, then walked slowly back to his friend. He broke a howl up into a series of quavering barks and stood over Don with slowly waving tail.

"Great Scott! I still can't believe it!" muttered Mr. Murray as he swung the canoe inshore with a twist of his paddle.

A moment later he and Judy were kneeling beside the unconscious boy while Lance pranced nervously about and whined and yelped his concern.

"Shouldn't we give him artificial respiration, Dad?" asked the white-faced Judy.

"No. He's breathing all right, but he's had a nasty thump on the head," said her father. "He must have dived into shallow water. If he doesn't come around soon, we'll have to get him back to camp some way."

In five minutes Don's eyes were open and he was weakly telling what he remembered of his story, while Lance sat watching him from a short distance.

Mr. Murray got the rifle from his canoe and fired the signal they had agreed upon to tell Mrs. Murray everything was all right. Lance dashed off along the shore with alert ears and came trailing back, disappointed that the shooting had brought him no food.

"Say, that dog is smart," said Mr. Murray admiringly. He stressed the word *dog* a little more than was necessary and Don caught the inflection.

"Now do you believe me?" he inquired with a smile.

"Not entirely," said his father. "But even if he's part wolf, there must be some dog in his ancestry not far back."

"There's a little wolf in every dog's ancestry, Dad!" Don insisted, in spite of his weakness.

Judy paddled out on the lake with her father to rescue the small canoe. The waves had flattened out with the falling wind and they had no trouble in bringing it back to shore. Don's fishing pole was still lodged under the thwarts. Lance showed an eager interest when he caught the scent of fish, and Don, poking about in the water in the bottom of the canoe, found one big bass still left of the string he had caught. The others must have retained enough life to wriggle free. Don tossed the fish to Lance, who downed it swiftly while the others watched in amazement.

"I suppose you'll be telling us all summer about the big ones who got away," complained Judy.

Don laughed and pointed to Lance. "This is the big one who didn't get away."

Don and his father started back to camp in the large canoe and Lance followed along quite willingly on shore.

Judy complained about having to paddle the soggy smaller craft but her father insisted. "No exercise for a couple of hours for Don. That submersion might be troublesome. It's always hard on the heart," he explained. "Anyhow, we have only two paddles now."

"Another thing, Sis," added Don. "You'd better get in first and tie up that crazy mutt of yours before he commits suicide."

That idea seemed to convince Judy and she paddled on ahead without any further objections. Don and his father went more slowly to make sure that Lance would follow them. A short distance from camp, the boy insisted on getting out to coax the young wolf along. Lance seemed less skittish than he had ever been before; he walked quietly along beside Don right into the cabin clearing. There he looked curiously about at the familiar surroundings with no sign of nervousness. He had watched the family for so long that he felt no fear of any of them.

Mrs. Murray admired him from a cautious distance. Lance made it plain that he did not like to be touched or patted, except occasionally by the boy, and even Don respected his natural dignity and independence.

They had a gala supper outdoors that night with Lance, as the guest of honour, receiving a whole steak for his share. The kerosene refrigerator was empty after the meal, but the day had to be marked in some memorable way.

"It'll be five days before we get any fresh meat," said Mrs. Murray, "but we owe a lot to Lance."

The squalling Jitters, locked in the cabin, was the only member of the family who did not pay his respects to the great wolf dog. The little cocker yapped his objections to everything that went on until even Judy was disgusted with him.

The rivalry between the two dogs was the main topic of camp discussion for the following week. Jitters had to be tied or locked up constantly, because he made it abundantly clear that as soon as he was free he would do his best to annihilate the burly wolf dog. He had never forgotten that the huge stranger had fled from him once in the woods, and he was convinced that he could put him to flight again.

Judy had to bring out the little dog's leash, and there were no more happy jaunts for him into the woods on the cold trails of rabbits and squirrels. He languished in yelping discontent, tied to a corner of the cabin, his unrest increased by the freedom of the big wolf dog.

Don was delighted to have his big pet back again and he lost no time in renewing his friendship. He began to teach him the game of the thrown stick and worked slowly up to simple commands like "Fetch!" and "Sit!" On the third day he actually induced Lance to join him, a bit nervously, in the canoe moored to the dock.

All this was like salt on the wounded pride of Jitters, who watched constantly for a chance to show his mettle.

Early one morning he found his opportunity. Don had got up and padded to the door in his pyjamas to have a look at the weather. When he unlatched the door and stepped out for a minute, it seemed warm enough for a swim, so he went back to don his trunks and join Lance, waiting at the float.

Jitters, usually asleep under Judy's bed, had one eye open and glimpsed his chance. Don returned a moment later to see the tiny spaniel dash out of the door and gallop madly down the path, yelping his battle cry.

Lance, on the float, was obviously uneasy. He paced back and forth as the tiny whirlwind approached and dashed along the plank at him. In the split second when the spaniel leaped forward, the wolf dog side-stepped nimbly and his tiny antagonist dived at full speed into the chilly waters of the lake.

Jitters was undaunted. He rose to the surface in hysterical anger and circled back to land, swimming manfully. He scrambled ashore and dashed for the plank walk again, barking his wrath in a series of shrill yaps.

Lance awaited the attack with dignity, but Jitters was too clever to be caught a second time by the same tactics. He circled the bigger animal for a moment and then drove in to snap at his legs. Lance leaned over and gripped the spaniel's harness in his teeth. He lifted him clear of the float and, with head held high, walked to the edge and dropped the little fellow into the water again.

Jitters paddled gamely ashore and returned to the

attack while the awakened family watched in an ecstasy of laughter. When Jitters charged him, Lance used the same defence, and Jitters found himself ducked in the lake for the third time.

Once more the gritty little spaniel rushed the wolf dog and once more he wound up in the lake. He struggled ashore at last in dignified silence and panted up the bank in dripping exhaustion. Ignoring all offers of sympathy, even from his beloved Judy, he trailed to a hole he had dug under the cabin and retired in silence. Not even his tin plate of breakfast could lure him out.

By the middle of the morning Judy was really worried and she appealed to Don for help. She didn't get any sympathy.

"Let him miss a few meals," growled Don. "He's too fat anyway."

But Judy received help from an unexpected quarter. Lance seemed to miss his small persecutor. Finally he walked over to the hole and peered in with his head set inquiringly on one side. He gave a friendly whine and sniffed.

A ferocious growl was the only answer that came from the darkness.

Lance set off purposefully into the woods and was gone for half an hour. When he returned he carried the limp body of a red squirrel dangling from his mouth. He laid the peace offering before the hole and cocked his ears for an answer to his overture.

Jitters growled again.

Lance sat for a moment as though in thought and then trotted off into the woods once more. He was gone much longer this time and when he returned he was breathing hard, but he carried another offering in his mouth. This one was a small brown rabbit.

He laid·it beside the squirrel and waited hopefully. All summer Jitters had been following the trails of rabbits, never with any success and often in the wrong direction. But the spaniel had been undiscouraged; he ran the trails until his drooping ears were soaked with dew and tangled with burrs, and he never lost heart.

Now he had his rabbit. Jitters thrust his small nose out and sniffed carefully. Then he crawled out all the way and pounced on the limp body with a ferocious growl. He glared around as though someone were plotting to take his rightful prey from him and finally carried it off into the bushes to gloat over it.

All the rest of the day he carried the rabbit around with him and managed to leave it where everyone could see it at one time or another. He would drop it as though he had forgotten about such a trifling matter as a rabbit, and wait for someone to come by. Thereupon he would leap fiercely on the limp form and glare at the intruder as though daring him to fight for the tattered game. At bedtime he tried to carry the badly shopworn rabbit into the house, but Mrs. Murray put her foot down. Jitters left the battered body outside of the door, and it was quietly disposed of as soon as he was out of sight.

The incident made a difference in Jitters; it restored his faith in the belief that rabbit tracks did lead somewhere after all. And it patched up the difficulties with Lance. From them on they were pals. They would play together and doze side by side in the sun. Lance made an effort to teach Jitters the skills of tracking, but it was useless. The spaniel continued to chase rabbits the wrong way until the day he left camp.

Two days later Mr. McLaren came in from the mine, packing in a new supply of fresh meat and guiding a schoolmate of Judy's who had flown up to spend a week with her. Lance was exhibited and admired, much to his discomfort, and he was very happy when Judy and Carla retired to the cabin to exchange gossip and the men went in for a swim.

Lounging on the float between dips, Don asked Mr. McLaren for an honest opinion about Lance. Was he a wolf or was he a dog?

"That's an awfully hard question, Don," said Mr. McLaren. "Let's put it this way. He looks like a dog, but so do most wolves; on the other hand he acts like a dog, and that's something that very seldom happens with a wolf. If one is caught and tamed as a very young puppy and brought up with dogs, it will act just like a dog—most of the time. But this fellow must have been a year old when you met him. The fairest answer would be just this: I don't know. But he's certainly more dog than wolf."

Don thought it over a long time and then brought out the question that had been really troubling him. "Do you think I can tame him, Mr. McLaren?"

"Tame him?" asked the mine manager in surprise. "Why, he's tame now!"

"I mean can I take him back to the city? Can I train him so he won't run away at the sight of an aeroplane or of people he isn't used to?"

"Well, if I were you I'd start right away. Day after to-morrow I'm going back to the mine. Why not hike in with me and bring Lance along? You can stay an hour or so and let him see other people, maybe watch a plane take off, and then come right back. Then every week you can bring him up to the mine again for a while and get him used to staying longer and longer."

"That's it!" Don slapped his hand on the planking. "I'll do that."

He got to his feet, feeling much better, and dove into the water.

Next morning the men decided to go fishing and, since there were three of them, Lance had to be left at home. He watched sadly as the canoe paddled out to the centre of the lake. Then he returned to loll in the shade of the cabin.

Judy and Carla set out for a stroll with Jitters, and Lance trailed halfheartedly along. They walked north for nearly a mile and finally settled themselves to rest where tall pines overhung the lake and a carpet of pine needles covered a high bank. It was cool and very still.

The woods behind them were dark and deep, and Lance looked forward to some pleasant squirrel hunting. He had not counted, however, on the doubtful assistance of Jitters. After his careful stalking had been ruined several times by the noisy intervention of the spaniel, he gave up. A quiet thicket offered a pleasant spot for a nap; he curled up on the soft forest carpet and drowsed off.

The girls talked for a while until Carla, overcome by the unaccustomed northern air, grew drowsy and fell asleep. Judy nodded sleepily over the book she had brought along. Only Jitters remained awake; he pattered busily to and fro through the woods, snuffling restlessly at the cold trails of squirrels and deer mice.

A cool wind blew from the mossy depths of the trees, and from far in the shadows of the forest came a wandering Canada lynx. Three hundred yards off its keen eyes spotted the aimless wanderings of the little black spaniel, who seemed to the lynx an odd shape for a fox but obviously something to be killed and eaten. The big cat crept closer with its spraddling, clumsy gait.

Judy and Carla slept on. Jitters, with his drooping ears trailing like blinkers, followed his busy nose across the forest floor. Lance dozed in his thicket; he lay like a silver-grey statue except for his alert nostrils which widened from time to time.

The lynx, more than twice the size of the little dog, slipped closer on its padded feet. It scanned the ground ahead and took advantage of every tree as cover. Twenty feet from the unsuspecting Jitters, it tucked its long hind legs under it for a spring, its stub of a tail twitching nervously.

Suddenly Jitters looked up. Though rabbits occupied his thoughts during the vacation, cats were his hobby at all other times. A thousand defeats had never shaken his confidence that he could conquer any cat that ever lived. The huge lynx was just another tabby to him. He yelped defiance and charged it without a moment's hesitation.

The sudden dash upset the lynx's plan; its leap carried it clear over the head of the advancing dog. Carla woke suddenly and looked up as the tufted-eared cat sailed through the air, fifty feet away. She gave a piercing shriek that further unsettled the lynx, but it was unwilling to forego a meal unless it had to. It wheeled and crouched for the spring again as Jitters skidded on the turn in his effort to follow the cat's movements.

Judy started out of her nap and joined her shrill screams to Carla's as the lynx sprang through the air again at Jitters. The noise they made and the mad scrambling of the spaniel combined to spoil the second attack. Once more the lynx overjumped its prey. It sprang three feet up a tree trunk and clung there, yowling and spitting.

Lance had opened his eyes lazily at the girls' first cries.

He was not unduly disturbed. He had noticed that the girls were always making unusual sounds which had no particular meaning. The caterwauling of the lynx was something else. It brought him to his feet, fully awake. He slid noiselessly out of his thicket and found himself in a perfect position to attack the great cat from the rear. He took two strides forward and jumped. His jaws gripped the lynx by the back of the neck and tore it from its foothold on the tree. It screeched once as he carried it with him to the ground. Then with a vicious shake of his head Lance broke its back and tossed it lifeless to the ground.

He looked up to see Judy and Carla disappearing through the trees with shrill cries of terror. They were going home much faster than they had come. He started to follow them but the urge to finish his interrupted nap was stronger than his curiosity.

Jitters was already growling furiously at the dead cat's body. It was too big for him to move, but he managed to get a grip on one hind leg and shake it a little. He let go of it and as it dropped, one limp sharp-pointed claw scratched his nose. He yelped and returned ferociously to worry its stub of a tail.

Lance watched him tolerantly for a moment and then sauntered back to his bed among the bushes.

The two girls stumbled into camp ten minutes later in a state of collapse; their legs were scratched and their dresses tattered by their wild flight through the brush.

D

"A panther!" Judy gasped. "He must have eaten up Jitters. Lance was fighting with him when we ran!"

The fishing party had just returned, and the men dropped their catch at once.

"That .22 won't be much good," said Mr. McLaren. "I left a carbine here last fall in the closet. We'd better take that."

They dug it out hastily, along with Mr. Murray's shotgun, and climbed into the larger canoe. The paddles flew as they set off for the scene of the attack.

There was not a sound as they drove the canoe ashore below the tall trees.

"If he's wounded, he'll be dangerous!" warned Mr. Murray. "The head and the spine are the places to aim. Let's spread out. Don, you keep in the middle, with that light gun."

They crept up the bank cautiously. There was nothing in sight. "This is the place, all right. There's Judy's book," said Mr. Murray.

"Here, Lance! Here, Lance!" called Don anxiously.

There was a rustle among the brush. Three guns were levelled as Lance strolled out, yawning hugely. He trotted slowly forward, blinking his eyes at the guns with interest.

"Where's Jitters?" asked Mr. Murray.

In answer the little dog came dashing from behind a tree and leaped up on them. He told the story of his fierce fight in a stream of yelps and excited whines.

Mr. McLaren strode forward to the tree and laughed aloud. "Here's your panther!" he called, as he started clicking shells from his rifle. "Just an alley cat!"

The others hurried up to examine the dead lynx.

"Pretty big for an alley cat!" commented Mr. Murray.

"They're cowards," explained the mine manager. "They'd gobble up Jitters here in a minute, but they'd never attack a human being."

The spaniel charged in, renewing his attempts to tug the wildcat around. Lance yawned again and cocked his head tolerantly sideways as he watched the little dog.

Mr. McLaren lifted up the cat and examined it under the yelping supervision of Jitters. "The fur isn't bad for this time of the year," he commented. "It would make a nice souvenir if you wanted to tan it."

The two men returned to camp in the canoe. They took with them both the lynx and the small spaniel, who refused to be separated from his prey. Don and Lance tramped back through the woods.

Back at camp, Mrs. Murray refused to share the general view of the big cat's harmlessness. "Those are awfully big claws," she insisted. "I think he must be dangerous."

There was a steak for supper that night. Mrs. Murray explained that each portion was a little smaller than usual because she had also provided a share for Lance.

"Lucky dog!" said Mr. McLaren, with a heavy stress on the second word.

7. TRAINING AND A PICNIC

AFTER breakfast the next morning Don started back to the mine with the manager. They had planned to take only Lance with them, but when Jitters discovered by the scent that the hide of his lynx was being carried along, he insisted noisily on making the trip too.

"It might be a good idea," said Mr. McLaren. "Jitters knows his way around up there, and when Lance sees that the little fellow isn't frightened, it will be easier for him."

The hike was pleasant in the morning coolness of the woods and the dogs seemed to enjoy it thoroughly. Don was a little less happy. He considered the trip a test of whether Lance could get used to civilization, and he worried most of the way. As they approached the mining camp and its scents and sounds became noticeable, he watched Lance carefully. The big wolf dog showed a growing uneasiness and began to lag behind. It was here that Jitters helped a great deal. Lance watched him closely and seemed to gain some comfort from his lack of fear.

Finally they reached the sloping hillside a mile from camp where Lance had taken flight only a few months before. On that unhappy occasion the low-flying plane had been a mischance but this time they had a stroke of luck. As Lance fell back, stirred by some vague memory of his previous fright, Jitters stumbled upon a late covey of young grouse. At the sight of him, the tiny balls of feathers vanished from sight and the mother fluttered temptingly off with what looked like a crippled wing.

Jitters tore off in pursuit of her, as he was expected to do, and Lance, excited by the nearness of the bird, followed him in a mad scramble. The mother bird led the dogs a chase of some yards before she made a miraculously sudden recovery and flew strongly away.

Don and Mr. McLaren stood beside the trail, staring at the ground where the tiny birds had vanished. The manager laughed. "Do you think you can find any of them?"

"Why, sure!" said Don. "I saw one duck under those dead leaves." He stepped over and picked up the withered twig.

There was nothing to be seen. He ran his hand across the ground and rustled the leaves.

"Just like a shell game, isn't it?" Mr. McLaren smiled.

"After my first few attempts, I stopped looking for them. It's like magic."

"But they must be here somewhere."

"Of course they are! There's the proof now." Mr. McLaren pointed to the father bird, clucking among the spruces behind them.

"Maybe the dogs could have found them if they'd been smart enough to stay and look," suggested Don.

"Only by luck. The little cusses don't have any scent until they get to be pretty big."

They continued their journey while the dogs scouted happily through the woods ahead of them. Another test came as they approached the edge of the big camp. A workman was clearing brush around one of the approach lights for the air strip, and Lance stopped dead at the sight of him. Jitters was undismayed; he dashed forward and leaped up in his usual friendly manner. The man stopped his work to pat him and tug his ears. Then Lance relaxed and waved his tail slowly back and forth.

When they reached the main part of the mine, Jitters was kept busy dashing back and forth to renew his acquaintance with everyone, and Lance followed him more slowly. He did not show any signs of fear, but seemed to be astonished that there were so many people in the world.

Finally the spaniel remembered Lance and led him off among the buildings. Don followed Mr. McLaren to his office shack.

"There's a little mail here for you people, and there'll be a big plane taking off in forty-five minutes. We'll see how Lance takes it. That'll give us time to get something to eat." The mine manager led the way to the mess hall.

The dogs had reached there ahead of them and were busily engaged in polishing off a couple of tin plates. The cook stood watching them. "That's what this camp needs," he said. "A couple of dogs around the place. Is that big fellow yours, son?"

Don nodded proudly.

"There's nothing like a German Shepherd for a man's dog," said the cook. "You can see that fellow's a thoroughbred. Worth a stack of chips, too, I'll bet!"

"There isn't enough money in Canada to buy him!" said Don.

For fifteen minutes he devoted himself to a smoking plate of ham and beans. Over the apple pie, he mentioned the subject of the aeroplane take-off.

"Well, this is what I think we ought to do," said Mr. McLaren. "We'll ask the pilot to come over and play with Jitters, pat him and talk to him, and then climb into the plane. That will give Lance the idea that there are men connected with all the noise and he won't be so frightened. Does it sound like a good idea to you?"

Don liked the idea. Half an hour later they stood on the runway watching the big plane with its motors ticking over slowly. Jitters played about, unaffected by the sight, but Lance hung back nervously.

The co-pilot waved an arm from the cabin and the pilot hurried out of the office.

"Well, so long, Mac! I'll see you next week, and you too, pup!" He bent down and pushed Jitters playfully around with one hand. "Want to come along?"

Jitters jumped up eagerly, quite willing to go. Don grabbed him back and stole a glance at Lance. The big wolf dog was watching everything carefully.

The pilot swung up into the ship and a moment later it taxied away from them down to the end of the air strip. It turned slowly and dust billowed up as the engines were revved up to a thunderous roar. They died down and the plane began to move back toward them.

The sound of the motor was deafening, but Jitters yelped delightedly and tried to tug loose from Don's grip. Lance watched the smaller dog and looked up nervously from time to time at the approaching plane.

As the big DC-3 swept past with its wheels lifted from the ground, Don released Jitters. He dashed after the flying plane with a volley of barks and Lance trotted uncertainly after him for only a moment before he, too, broke into a run. If this was a game, he wasn't going to be left out of it. The plane disappeared over the trees and the two dogs galloped back. Lance played about with Jitters, all trace of nervousness apparently gone.

Don turned to Mr. McLaren. "I guess your plan worked all right."

"If there's any credit, I think you'd better give it to Jitters. We'd never have put it over without him," said the manager.

"Now my next problem is to get Lance to wear a collar," said Don. "How do you think he'll feel about it?"

"I can tell you right now he won't like it. But you've got to start some time, I suppose."

Back in the camp at the lake, Don devoted an hour or more every day to the education of Lance. He remembered the commands used in obedience training and the wolf dog picked up the idea quickly. It seemed a little silly in the deep woods to teach him "Heel!" and "Sit, stay!" and the rest, but Don thought of the city life to come and worked hard at it. Lance was a pleasure to teach, and the swims and romps that followed the lessons were all the reward he asked.

But the collar was a different matter; Lance seemed to have a strong dislike for anything that bound him tightly. Don began with an old handkerchief, laying it lightly across the wolf dog's neck. Lance didn't like it but made no attempt to get rid of it. But the first time Don knotted it loosely around his neck he leaped away, shaking his head nervously. He rolled on the ground, rubbing at the offending handkerchief until it came loose; then he seized it in his teeth and whipped it back and forth with fierce shakes of his head as a puppy shakes a piece of rope.

Don wisely dropped the idea and went back to the obedience training. Lance liked that and grew more attentive day by day. He enjoyed especially the "Don't touch!" training with a piece of meat, because the meat was always his reward for a good performance.

Don slipped into his place at the supper table one evening after a run with Lance and found the family in the midst of an argument.

"You simply cannot go away out there alone," Mrs. Murray was insisting. "Remember what happened the last time you girls went out together, and that was only a mile away."

"But that would never happen again," said Judy.

"You are not going alone anyway," answered her mother.

"Do you think we'd be safe if Lance went along, Mrs. Murray?" asked Carla.

"Now wait a minute!" put in Don. "Who says you can take Lance?"

"Donald!" warned his mother. "Carla is Judy's guest."

"But gosh, Mum, Lance is my dog!"

"The girls want to have a picnic across the lake," explained Mr. Murray. "And I think you should let them take Lance if they need him."

"Oh, a picnic!" exclaimed Don as he loaded his plate generously. "What are you going to have to eat?"

"Listen to that, Mother," said Judy scornfully. "He's trying to blackmail us now."

Mrs. Murray remained tactfully silent, letting nature take its course.

"We're going to have lettuce-and-tomato sandwiches," said Judy reluctantly.

"And?" suggested Don.

"Oh, hot dogs and marshmallows, I suppose."

"And maybe some home-made fudge and that box of candy Carla brought you?" suggested Don with a grin.

"Mother!" complained Judy. "You see what he's doing?"

"Now, Judy," soothed Mrs. Murray, "if you invite Don and Lance to your picnic you should have something they like, too."

Next morning after breakfast the picnic party started off across the lake in both canoes. Carla and Judy took all the supplies in the larger canoe, since Don insisted that the smaller one was barely large enough for him and Lance. He wanted to do some fishing and the big canoe was too unhandy for that. They landed on a woody point which Judy had often admired from the canoe dock, and she and Carla spent an hour or two picking flowers under the escort of Lance and Jitters. Don piled up stones for a fireplace and laid the wood for cooking.

The meal was a great success. After everything but the last of the fudge had been finished, Don pocketed that and announced he was going fishing. He paddled out a hundred yards and began casting at a likely bass spot, while Lance sat erect on the bank watching every move intently. The girls looked on until the monotony palled on them and they began to doze. Jitters curled himself up to dream of rabbits.

The remains of the lunch no longer had any attraction for them, but to a furry little animal half a mile away the scent promised a welcome change of diet. A slow-footed skunk smelled the food and recognized something tastier than the grubs and beetles he was dislodging from an overturned log.

He was a beautiful little animal with a white spot on his nose and a larger white tip to his tail; the rest of his body was a glossy black except for a broad white V that ran down across his shoulders. Left to himself, he was a harmless and attractive little creature who could be approached and even fed without any unpleasant results. When worried or disturbed, he made a nuisance of himself.

He sniffed the food from a distance and came waddling toward it with quiet dignity. At the border of the open glade he stopped and looked carefully around. There was the food, all right, and no one was in sight. He ambled softly forward and began to eat. If all had gone well, he would have dined and departed as quietly as he had come, and no one would have been any the wiser.

Unfortunately, Carla awoke and stretched idly. She remembered the huge bouquet of woods flowers that she and Judy had gathered. Perhaps she had better dip the stems in water to keep them from withering. She got to her feet and walked a few steps into the woods, then stopped, horror-stricken at the sight of the intruder. She was a city girl and had no idea of the etiquette which the occasion required. Ducking hastily behind a tree, she screamed. The polite skunk began a slow and dignified retreat, but it was not quick enough for Carla.

"Judy!" she called. "Jitters! Sic 'em!"

Jitters leaped wildly out of his slumber and stared at the intruder. Back in his puppyhood he had committed one indiscretion connected with a skunk and the incident had left its mark on his sensitive soul. He growled softly and began backing hastily into the brush.

"Lance!" cried Carla in despair. "Lance! Sic 'em!"

The wolf dog leaped up the bank at the sound of his name and took a look at the skunk. Judy awoke and stared around wildly. She saw nothing, but automatically she echoed her friend's cries.

"Sic 'em, Lance!" she called earnestly.

Lance advanced with great distaste. The skunk turned his back on the dog menacingly. Lance circled quickly to get in front of him. The skunk turned again, and Lance danced around him once more. They drew closer to each other, both circling desperately. Lance realized that he was covering much more ground than his slower opponent and was doomed to lose the dizzy race. Lifting his upper lip in disgust, he dived in and seized the circling skunk. A quick flirt of his head, and the harmless little animal had joined his forefathers; but in death he had his revenge. His last unconscious act was a quick upward flip of his tail. Only one drop of the two or three which he ejected landed on Lance, but that was far too much.

Fifty feet out on the lake and paddling madly for shore, Don sniffed, and roared out his disgust. "What have you kids got into now?" he demanded, as he grounded the canoe and dashed up the bank.

There was no need to answer the question. Lance approached him slowly, with his head down and swinging from side to side sheepishly. He was miserable.

"Oh, my gosh!" snorted Don. "You girls don't need a dog; you need a baby sitter! Why, you haven't the sense. . . . Here, boy! Here, boy!" He broke off to soothe the crestfallen dog.

For once Lance was not aloof and distant. He felt that he had made a fool of himself and wanted patting and reassurance. All he had done was to follow orders. Both girls had cried, "Sic 'em!" and he had done their bidding.

Carla and Judy, with handkerchiefs to their noses, were deeply repentant but, as Don pointed out, that wasn't going to wash Lance. They embarked for camp with Don transporting the unhappy wolf dog. The two girls made no objection at all to carrying the rest of the supplies; Judy even offered, very humbly for her, to take along Don's fishing rod and creel.

When he reached the cabin, Don was delighted to find

that his mother had planned to do some washing. A big tub of water was warming in the glaring sun on the terrace. That would come in handy. He stuck his head in the screen door.

"Hey, Mum! I need this tub of water to wash Lance," he called. "And I want a tin of tomatoes, too. A big tin!" He remembered the procedure that he had used to make Jitters acceptable in polite society again.

"You don't need anything of the kind!" said his mother indignantly. "I've been waiting all day for that water to get warm. And tomatoes? Do you realize, young man, that every tin of food has to be carried out here on somebody's back?"

She came to the door, wiping her hands on her apron, just as Lance approached. A random breeze flitted through the clearing and Mrs. Murray changed her mind quickly. "By all means use the water, Don," she said as she backed away. "Will one tin of tomatoes be enough?"

Don went busily to work massaging Lance with the tomatoes, which seemed to have a magical ability to absorb and neutralize the acrid musk of the skunk's weapon. Mr. Murray wandered out to watch the process, but soon retreated.

"I thought you said that you didn't mind that skunk smell, Dad," joked Don.

"I said it was rather pleasant at a distance," retorted his father. "And I meant *distance!* This is a little too close to home."

Don was hard at work when the girls arrived and landed their canoe. They walked quietly up to the cabin, anxious to avoid any discussion of their error of judgment.

But Don was not one to let the opportunity pass. "Ah! The young pioneers of the north woods!" he taunted. "And how did the nature study go to-day? Been picking wild flowers, I see. Poison ivy, no doubt!"

"Gee, I'm sorry, Don!" said Judy with unusual mildness. "I honestly am. I was in a fog!"

"But it was really my fault!" insisted Carla. "I'll make some fudge for you and Lance."

In half an hour the big dog was almost presentable again. Don rubbed him dry with an old towel and lounged in the sun with him afterward. A sudden idea struck him. He rushed into the house for a piece of strap from his knapsack and an old hairbrush. Lance had enjoyed being scrubbed with the soap after the tomatoes had been rinsed off, so possibly he would like a thorough brushing and grooming. It was a good guess; he showed his pleasure with a waving tail, and after some minutes of brushing he made no objection when Don looped the strap around his neck like a collar.

The boy praised his looks in a steady flow of admiring words as he brushed. After he had finished, Lance took an almost childish pleasure in strolling around to be admired by all the members of the household. He so far forgot his aloofness as to brush against people's legs until they noticed him and praised his appearance and his collar.

8. CRASH LANDING

LIFE at the camp settled into a pleasant routine. The days begin to shorten a little, although the daylight still lasted until after nine o'clock and the sun was up before the earliest riser in the little group. Mornings were chillier and often the mist rose from the lake like a white cloud.

By mid-morning the days were as warm and pleasant as they had been in early summer and there were only the splotches of autumn colour to show that it was not July. In a dozen places around the edge of the lake whole branches of the maple trees were brilliant red and the tops of the beeches were turning a sunny yellow.

At night a loon wailed his shuddering laugh across the darkness of the lake, and the katydids clacked their endless dialogues in the black woods. Often the northern lights would slant and shift and shimmer over half the sky, like great batteries of coloured searchlights fading and strengthening beyond the hills to the north.

Don made his regular trips to the mine every four or five days with Lance and Jitters. The dogs looked forward to it and their first call on every visit was at the door of the mess hall.

"Only customers we have that don't complain about the food!" said the cook, who had taken a special liking to Lance.

Carla left to rejoin her parents at a seashore resort in New England, and Judy and Jitters went with her for a few weeks. The camp was very quiet after they left; Don and Lance lazed and tramped and fished with no interruptions. The training went forward as usual, with Lance seeming more like a real dog now that he wore a collar.

The only trace of his wild life was the way he felt about a house. It still seemed to bother him to spend much time under a roof. He would come in when called and he would go anywhere in the house that Don went, but he would never lie down for more than a moment. When it came time for bed, he always returned to the open air. Even on nights when rain slashed at the windows and thrummed on the roof and a cheerful fire burned in the open fireplace, Lance refused to stay. He would sleep in the open shed or under an overturned canoe, but that was all the roof he could endure.

One crisp evening Don sat late on the float with Lance, watching for the moonrise. There was a smell of frost in the air and not a breath of wind was stirring. He could hear the moaning of the little owls in the swamp a mile away and the occasional splash of a leaping fish.

When the silver disk of the moon finally rose above the black outline of the hills, Don was stiff and cold. He leaned over and patted Lance. "Good night, boy!" he said.

The wolf dog snorted out of a drowse and thumped his tail in reply. He heaved a long sigh and stretched himself to sleep again on the cold planks.

Don tramped up the path to the unlighted cabin. His father and mother were asleep and he let himself in quietly. As he drowsily undressed in the darkness, he thought with a touch of sadness that Lance was still pretty wild if he preferred to sleep outdoors on a night like this. In five minutes he was asleep.

It must have been several hours later when he suddenly found himself standing wide awake on the cold floor. He listened. There was a soft whine from Lance and an impatient scratching at the cabin door. Don thrust his feet into his chilly moccasins and hurried out to him.

The big dog stood alert and nervous in the bright moonlight. When he saw the boy he turned quickly and trotted down the path to the lake. Don followed him, shivering in the keen air, to the float, where Lance stood staring out across the lake with ears erect. A light mist was smoking up from the water and the black outlines of the trees in the moonlight were as clear-cut as scenery on a stage.

Don listened for a moment before he heard, faint and far off, the drone of an aeroplane motor. That was strange! The planes from the mine never got out as far as this. As he listened, the drone broke into the pup-pa-pup of a motor that was missing badly; then the steady beat began again. He searched the sky for the plane's riding lights but there was nothing to be seen.

The drone was suddenly louder. He caught sight of the red and green dots of light as they showed over the trees, perilously low across the wide lake. Even with the moonlight it would be tricky to land a seaplane at night on the misty water. He peered into the distance, and suddenly his heart sank. The flitting silhouette of the tiny plane against the moon showed the slim outline of a wheeled landing gear! The mine's landing strip was the only place where that fellow could get down safely.

Again the motor beat popped and missed and the tiny plane swung dangerously low. Then the motor stopped altogether. Don clenched his hands and tightened his muscles as he leaned forward for the inevitable crash.

The motor caught again and sparks fluttered from the exhaust as the plane lifted above the mist. Don could imagine the last few cupfuls of petrol sloshing back and forth in the empty tank. The plane rose strongly for several minutes, heading south toward the second lake. Don wanted to call out to the pilot, but he knew how useless that would be. If only he had brought his flash-light—but it was too late for anything now!

The drone grew fainter as the plane scudded on down the length of the chain of lakes, fighting for a little altitude. The wing-tip lights were almost lost among the stars, but still the steady drone hummed on. Did it stop? Or had it just flown out of hearing? A sharp backfire, and then silence, and the riding lights went down at a steep angle into the mist.

There was no explosion. Not enough petrol for that, thought Don. He turned back to the cabin, suddenly tired by the strain. Maybe a man was dead down there in a smashed plane in the dark woods. Or maybe he was struggling for life in the cold black water of the lake.

His father met him at the door, rubbing sleep from his eyes. "What's the matter, Don? I heard you get up."

Don told him what he had seen.

They lighted a lamp and sat down at the kitchen table while Lance stood looking from one to the other.

Mr. Murray reached over and patted him absently. "Good boy! you knew it was something unusual." He turned to Don. "Six or eight miles, eh? That's a good two hours by canoe. You'll have to take Lance to help you find . . . whatever's to be found. I'd rather make the trip myself, but Lance takes his orders from you. I'll go to the mine. Maybe they can locate a seaplane somewhere by radio and send it over. But we'll have to wait until daylight."

"If he's in the lake, I might help him if I started now,"

urged Don. It seemed so heartless to be sitting there and doing nothing.

His father shook his head. "You couldn't see a quarter of a mile through the mist once you got out there. You might miss him altogether. At daybreak you can start out in the canoe, and I'll get on to the mine."

Lance got up and walked over to nose the screen door open.

With a sigh Don got to his feet. "I don't think I can sleep any more," he said heavily. "Might as well get some stuff together for the trip."

Silently he and his father made their preparations for the morning's start. They folded blankets in a poncho and looked over their scanty first-aid supplies. Mrs. Murray had awakened and moved quietly around, making an occasional suggestion as she set out dishes for a quick breakfast. In half an hour there was nothing left to do but wait for daylight.

"Better turn in, son," advised Mr. Murray. "Even if you can't sleep, the rest will do you good. You have a hard day ahead."

Don nodded and went back to his room with sagging shoulders. He pulled the blankets over him and lay for a long time staring at the ceiling.

The next thing he knew, the room was grey with the light of dawn and the alarm clock was burring in his father's room. He got up and dressed hastily. Breakfast was hissing on the stove as he walked into the kitchen.

He and his father ate rapidly, speaking only an occasional word about plans or suggestions.

"If that fellow is badly hurt, don't try to move him alone," advised his father.

Don nodded absently. "Better warn the seaplane pilot about those sunken logs on the west shore of the second lake. He'll have to land far out and taxi in slowly," he said.

His father nodded. "No stimulant if there are any head injuries, remember!" he warned.

They pushed their chairs back at the same moment and began to gather up the kit for the canoe. Lance was waiting outside and padded beside them down to the float. They ran the canoe into the water and loaded it carefully from the dock. Lance let himself delicately down into it, stepping in the exact centre and well forward.

At the last minute, Mrs. Murray hurried down with a thermos bottle of hot coffee. She handed it down to Don, who stowed it away among the folded blankets under the thwarts.

"Be careful!" warned his mother as he pushed out into the mist-veiled lake.

"Don't take any chances!" called his father.

The sun was a pale outline through the fog as Don paddled out into the moist white dimness. The wind was beginning to stir the thin clouds and already the smooth surface of the water was clearing. In five minutes he was out of sight of any shore, but he kept the dim sun over his left shoulder and paddled ahead as confidently as if he could see his destination before him.

The laden canoe was heavier than he was used to and the work was hard, but the weight gave the craft momentum and, once under way, it cut whisperingly through the water. Farther out on the lake the wind had scoured the fog from the surface. Don got a glimpse of blue sky overhead. The trailing curtains of mist were driven before the breeze like smoke and the water glistened brightly. It was a fine morning but he could not enjoy it. He leaned into his paddle grimly, weighed down by the unknown possibilities that lay ahead.

The narrow passage into the second lake was lightly veiled in mist, but Don's navigation had been faultless and he hit it exactly. He lifted his paddle and rested it across the gunwales as the canoe coasted through the narrow channel. From here on he would have to look around carefully for signs of the wrecked plane. If it had landed on the water, the pilot had a chance. If it had come down in the woods, there wasn't much hope for him. A quarter mile in from the lake, and the wreck might not be found for weeks.

Don cut in closer to the shore and peered carefully through the mist as the tall trees slid past him. He swung out again to circle a narrow point and then back again. For fifteen minutes he paddled slowly along while the wooded shore cleared rapidly under the gusty wind.

There was nothing to be seen but tangled brush and tall trees. He rounded another point and suddenly his heart pounded excitedly. A pair of jays had flown up from the woods, squawking raucously, and high on a tree behind them he saw the bright yellow strip where a branch had been recently broken. He swung the canoe in toward shore and searched for a landing spot. Up front, Lance lifted first one forepaw and then the other in nervous anticipation.

A sandy stretch between two rocks looked good. Don drove the canoe a foot up on the shelving bank. Lance looked inquiringly over his shoulder, and Don waved him out. "Go, Lance!" he ordered, and the dog leaped lightly ashore.

Don followed more slowly, gripping the gunwales and stepping carefully over the piled kit amidships. The ground was firm and dry and he tugged the canoe up another foot before heading into the brush.

The thick bushes masked a rocky slope. Don crouched as he forced his way in, parting the tangled branches with his hands and sweeping spiders' webs aside. Lance followed close behind. At the top of the little rise they looked into a swampy glade, thick with berry bushes. There was no sign of the plane, and a closer look at the scarred tree showed the wood dry and weathered. Don was about to turn back when a rustle among the bushes reached his ear.

"Hello!" he called. The bushes shook and parted as a

half-grown bear peered out at them a hundred feet away. Lance growled and started forward. The bear snatched a last pawful of berries and went down on all fours to dash away.

"Heel, Lance!" ordered Don. The dog stopped and looked at him in surprise before obeying with lowered head.

They slid down the slope to the shore of the lake. Don patted the downcast dog before climbing back into the canoe. "What would you do with the bear if you caught him?" he asked, smiling.

Pushing out again, he continued the slow examination of the shore line. Another fruitless mile brought him to the end of the second lake and the passage into the third of the little chain. This was farther than he had expected to go. It didn't seem possible that the plane could have got this far; he began to fear it had crashed somewhere deep in the woods behind him.

The mist was gone now and the sun was warm. Broken clouds were coming in from the east, but the wind was still dry. Don wriggled carefully out of his sweat shirt and tossed it forward in the canoe. He began to feel hungry and he suddenly realized it was nearly noon. He decided to push on into the third lake before eating. He had not been down this far since the day that Lance pulled him out of the water after the canoe capsized. He paddled hard through the narrow strait and then leaned back to watch as the canoe coasted out into the wide lake.

Suddenly all thoughts of food or rest vanished from his mind. A mile away across the lake the silver tail of a plane jutted starkly above the still water. There was not a sound or a sign of life around. He dipped his paddle furiously and the canoe hissed through the quiet water. Lance raised his head to sniff the air and whimpered softly.

In less than ten minutes they were close up. The plane was a good hundred yards out from the west shore, which sloped steeply down to the edge of the lake. The water must be deep there. Don swung away as he approached; the plane might be balanced on a sunken log or a big underwater rock. He did not want to take a chance of dislodging it. It might swing either way and trap the canoe under the branching tail. He thought for a moment of beaching the canoe, swimming out, and diving to discover whatever he could. But he decided against it after circling the wreck at a safe distance. Shoreward the long trailers from weed beds waved up to within a few feet of the surface. That was dangerous stuff to get tangled in!

He ventured a little closer and peered down into the yellow-green water. He could not see much more than a yard down and he shuddered to think of the pilot probably still trapped down there in the cold darkness. He must have dived straight in through the night mist. Dejectedly Don circled the plane to look for any floating clues. Something caught his eye. The underside of the tail was dented and battered. If the plane had dived in, the tail would be unharmed.

Certainly! That was it. When you ditched a plane you were supposed to level off as low as you dared and then pull up the nose so the tail would hit first and the plane would slap in without diving. This one must have floated a while before going down. If the pilot was conscious after the crash, he might have been able to swim ashore.

Don swung the canoe around and headed for the rocky bank. A landing place was easy to find, but there was no spot flat enough to beach the canoe. Finally he knotted one sleeve of his sweat shirt to a thwart and tied the other to the branch of an overhanging tree. He waved Lance ashore while he steadied the canoe; then he carefully climbed out himself. Walking was difficult along the steep bank but he skirted the shore as closely as he dared, gripping bushes and trees to keep his balance. Lance leaped agilely on ahead, scouting up and down the slope as though glad to stretch his legs.

After covering two hundred yards of the shore line without finding a sign of anyone's having landed, Don began to fear his hope was vain. Perhaps the pilot had been knocked out by the crash. Perhaps he had even headed the wrong way in the mist and swum out into the miles of open lake.

Then Lance began to bark excitedly at the water's edge far ahead. Don plunged forward with reckless abandon, slipping on mossy rocks and ducking under low branches.

The dog was far beyond the plane and close to the water. Scratched and breathless, Don reached him at last, to find him standing over a flat rock on the shore, deep in a clump of bushes. Across the stone lay a few strands of damp water weed and a blur of muddy footprints.

There was a spatter of brick-red stains on the stone. Before Don reached down to run his hand across the dried drops, he knew that they were blood.

9. LANCE TO THE RESCUE

DON raised his head and shouted. "Hello-o-o!" There was no sound from the silent shore. A full minute later a faint echo answered mockingly from across the lake. Lance sat back on his haunches and looked up questioningly.

"Find him!" ordered Don, slapping his hand on the stained rock and swinging an arm off toward the thick brush.

Lance sniffed the tracks and then turned eagerly up the hill with his nose to the ground. Don toiled after him. He could see no sign of a trail on the rocky slope but he followed the wolf dog confidently. The way led upward for nearly a hundred yards. Then the ground levelled off among tall trees that sheltered a wide belt of waist-deep fern. Don plunged forward through the heavy growth, following Lance by the stirring of the ferns above him. There was still no sign of a trail.

As they went on, the ground gradually cleared. In patches where the growth was thin, Don could see an occasional overturned mossy stone showing that someone had passed. Lance was right; his infallible nose had led him along a trail that no one else could have found. They pushed on faster through easy open ground. The land dipped down into a grove of higher trees where no sunlight penetrated and scattered katydids talked back and forth almost as though it were night. Don shivered and began to wish he had stopped for something to eat. They must be nearly a mile from the lake by now. He stopped and shouted.

There was no answer, but somewhere a quail whistled. Lance began to bark excitedly and the quail whistled again. The wolf dog leaped eagerly up to stare around over the high growth of brush.

"Down, boy!" order Don impatiently. "Find him!" He swung his arm along the ground.

Lance barked once more and dashed forward at a pace that left the boy far behind. As Don started to run the quail whistled up ahead again. Strange, he thought; he had never heard quail around here before. It was even stranger that the call should have distracted Lance from his job.

A hundred yards ahead the dog howled. Don sprinted forward, panting, and burst into a clearing among the trees. The sun shone on hip-deep grass and in the midst of it Lance was leaping high to look for his master. Don, wading forward through the heavy growth, suddenly started back in surprise.

In a little trampled patch lay an unconscious man. The wet grass was crushed and matted under him. He must have been there a long time. His face was streaked with blood and his damp clothes were muddy. It was the pilot, all right. Lance stood over him, sniffing his face.

Don rushed forward and knelt beside him. He picked up a limp, cold hand, rubbed the wrist, and felt for a pulse.

The man opened his eyes, and a spasm of pain creased his face.

"Are you badly hurt?" asked Don, with Lance looking over his shoulder.

"Broken ribs," whispered the man. "Help me up."

Don slipped his arm under the man's shoulders and eased him forward. He sat up and pressed his hand hard against his side. A fit of shivering shook him until his teeth chattered and he fought to catch his breath.

"I couldn't shout when I heard you," he murmured painfully. "I whistled a few times, and when I took a deep breath to shout, the pain knocked me out."

"Can you walk?" asked Don. "I've got some food at the lake."

"I'm all right. But my friend"—his whisper was urgent—"he . . ." His eyes closed and he fell back against Don's arm.

Don could have kicked himself for not bringing the food. This looked like shock. First aid for that was warmth and a stimulant. That would be the blankets and coffee back in the canoe—and a lot of good they were doing there!

He lowered the man to the ground, chafed his wrists, and lifted his knees. That should help.

In a few minutes the man opened his eyes again.

"Get me up!" he breathed. "I'm freezing!"

"Stay where you are a minute!" urged Don. "Where's your friend?"

"The mine!" whispered the pilot faintly. "Went on to the mine!"

"What mine?" asked Don, puzzled.

"Map showed a mine," came the faint answer. "Three —four miles west of here."

Don whistled softly. "Gosh, you fellows were really lost."

There was a lake fifteen miles to the east, beyond the big mine. Going west from that lake a man would reach the mine. The fliers must have misread the map.

"There's no mine that way," said Don. "Nothing but woods and mountains."

The man's eyes closed. Don thought he had fainted, but it was just discouragement. "Find him!" he whispered. "I'll be all right. Go find him."

Don sat back on his heels to think. He couldn't leave this fellow and yet he couldn't allow the other man to wander off into the wilderness. He had a sudden inspiration. A note!

E

"What's your name?" he asked.

"Ted—Ted Hayes," the man faltered, as though exhausted.

"And your friend?" Don was searching his pockets.

"Jack Cushing."

Matches, jack-knife, bandanna handkerchief—nothing to write with. Don stared about and ran over to a birch tree. Stripping off a piece of bark, he searched his pockets again. Burnt matches might do. Ah, what was that? A .22 cartridge in the bottom of a side pocket. He pulled it out and with it printed hastily, "Jack—Follow the dog—Ted." Knotting the bark into his handkerchief, he tied the whole thing to Lance's collar.

He walked to the edge of the clearing with the dog, rubbing his ears affectionately. "Go, Lance! Fetch him!"

The dog whined and searched up and down the edge of the woods for a moment. He struck a trail and stopped to look back over his shoulder.

"Fetch him, boy!" repeated Don.

Lance barked once and set off alone into the deep woods.

Don knelt beside the pilot again. "The dog has gone after your friend," he explained. "I'm going back to get some food and blankets. Now don't try to get up and I'll be back as quick as I can."

Don got to his feet and set off for the lake at a trot. It seemed shorter going back, but he realized it was downhill and his return would be harder. In less than ten minutes he stood panting at the side of the canoe. He tugged it close to the bank and pulled out a blanket and the poncho. He bundled the thermos and the package of sandwiches into them and made a tight roll. After securing both ends with a loop of rope, he raised the burden to his shoulders and climbed back up the slope. Snapping twigs and tramping down ferns, he struggled along. It was slow going and he stopped twice to rest before he staggered into the grassy clearing.

The pilot had not moved. Don swung his pack down beside him, pulled out the thermos, and poured coffee into one of the cups nested in its cap. Kneeling beside the injured man, he helped him to sit up and held the hot drink to his lips.

After the man had swallowed some of it, a little colour came back into his face. When he was able to hold the cup himself, Don opened the package of sandwiches and set them beside the pilot. He drank some of his own coffee, stuffed half a sandwich into his mouth, and chewed hungrily while he unfolded the blanket and poncho.

"Now, Mr. Hayes, you'd better slide over on this," he directed.

He helped the man to get the blanket under him before he sat down to gulp the rest of his sandwich and coffee. Glancing sideways at the lunch, he decided he could take another sandwich and still leave enough for Hayes and for Cushing if Lance could find him.

He picked up the sandwich. "I'm going on after your

friend now," he said. "Leave the food and coffee here if
you feel strong enough to move, but don't go any
distance without that blanket. I've marked the way back
to the canoe and I hope my father will be able to send a
seaplane along to pick you up before dark. Good luck!"

He acknowledged the man's murmured thanks with a
gesture and started for the edge of the woods, but a quick
glance at the sky brought him back. "Look, Mr. Hayes.
It's clouding up a bit. If you start for the lake you'd
better take the poncho, too. Another wetting won't do
you any good."

Munching the sandwich, Don plunged into the woods.
He would have to be careful about this; the wolf dog
would leave no trail. He would have to watch for the
few marks left by the man named Jack. It was even
slower going now. The woods were darker and all he
could see were the very clearest signs; a footprint in a
damp place, a stone with moss scraped off, a crushed
plant. He paused every hundred feet or so to check his
direction and call to Lance. He was worried about the
weather, too. Occasional glances overhead showed a
slowly thickening cloud layer. There was no sign of rain
yet, but even a low overcast could hide the lake from the
eyes of a searching pilot.

Don pushed slowly forward, watching for the faint
signs of the trail and calling to Lance. After an hour he
figured he had gone scarcely more than a mile. At last
he stopped, bewildered. He had come a hundred yards

since the last faint footprint; he had circled and cast back and forth in vain. He called, and strained his ears for a reply. He dared go no farther without some clue as to the direction. Suddenly he raised his head. Was that a faint yelp? He stopped breathing to listen.

A gust of wind hummed through the pines overhead and two branches squeaked as they rubbed together. When the wind died away, the sound came again, clearer. He shouted at the top of his lungs. Lance's answer was a chorus of joyful barks.

Don plunged forward recklessly; he couldn't get lost now. In five minutes he saw the trotting figure of the wolf dog coming toward him through the tree trunks. Behind Lance a tall man hobbled painfully along.

"Hello there, Mr. Cushing!" Don shouted.

The man waved one arm. The other hung useless at his side. "Is this your dog?" he panted hoarsely, as Don came up. "He saved my life back there in the swamps. Did you find Hayes?"

Don explained where he had left the other man, while Lance leaped joyfully up on him. He patted him, staring in spite of himself at the newcomer's battered face.

Cushing managed a grin as he touched his swollen nose with a careful finger. "I must look pretty bad."

"It's mainly those two black eyes," said Don, turning toward the lake.

"Oh, yes. I forgot," said Cushing. "Always happens after a bang on the nose. How's Ted?"

"He seems pretty sick," said Don. "I don't know how long he was lying on the ground."

"He was at the controls," Cushing explained, as they moved ahead through the woods. "He really nursed the plane in, but the landing doubled him over the wheel. I was lucky. I slammed into the instrument panel, but at least I was able to keep moving."

"How's the arm?"

"Broken," said the man. "How much farther is that clearing?"

"Less than a mile," said Don, staring at the sky. "I hope the rain holds off."

They pushed on in silence. The big man was staggering with weariness but he did not complain. Don wanted to question him about his meeting with Lance in the swamp, but he decided to wait until he had had something to eat.

When at last they reached the clearing covered with deep grass, Ted was nowhere in sight. The bundle of lunch and the thermos were still there.

Cushing let himself down beside them with a deep sigh. "I can't open that thermos," he said, "but I can eat with one hand." He tore the wrapping from a sandwich with his teeth.

Don opened the thermos and poured out two cupfuls of coffee. He took half a sandwich for himself. A few drops of rain fell, whispering softly through the dark trees.

They ate in silence until suddenly Don exclaimed,

"Was that a plane?" From far off came the unmistakable sound of an aeroplane motor.

Don leaped to his feet. "We'd better be getting along. We'll have to help Ted on the plane. He'd have a tough time getting into the canoe alone, and the pilot may not get in very close."

Cushing swallowed the last crumb and gulped down the rest of his coffee. "That saved my life! It's twenty-four hours since I had anything but a few blackberries."

Don picked up the thermos bottle and they pushed forward into the last stretch of woods with Lance ranging ahead. The way was downhill and the thought of the waiting plane sustained them. The rain came down more heavily; before they glimpsed the dull gleam of the lake through the trees they were soaked. Only Lance seemed to enjoy the tramp.

As they slid through dripping bushes to the edge of the water, they saw the seaplane fifty feet out, with the canoe moored to it and an anxious pilot peering from the door.

"Let's go!" he yelled impatiently as he sighted them. "I've got one of your men aboard here. Who else is going?"

When he saw the battered Cushing, he did not wait for an answer but lowered himself into the canoe and paddled ashore. "I want to take off before the weather gets any thicker," he explained apologetically. "Can you get in all right, buddy? Your pal was dead weight."

Don helped the injured Cushing to clamber in, then turned to Lance. "Sit, stay!" he ordered.

The big wolf dog obeyed, whimpering as he saw his master lower himself into the heavily laden canoe. They boosted Cushing into the plane first. As the pilot followed him, Cushing called out to Don in the canoe, "I don't know how to thank you."

Don blushed. "I guess Lance should get any credit there is," he mumbled.

The pilot cut short any further conversation. "Stand off a bit, son. I'm going to spin that prop."

Don paddled clear as the starter whirred and the propeller hitched, spun, and disappeared into a whining circle. Lance yelped excitedly as the plane moved slowly out into the lake for the take-off.

Don paddled to shore, waved Lance aboard, and took stock of his position. It was nearly dusk. The blankets were soggy and the poncho shining wet. It was a long ten miles home and the rain was still coming down heavily. He was soaked through.

He looked out at the plane. It was gathering speed; the dripping floats rose heavily and the little ship lifted into the air. Don watched it labour out of sight into the overcast and then bent to his paddle. As he passed the submerged plane, there was a hiss of escaping air and the silver shape slipped a foot deeper into the water. He shivered and dug in his paddle.

The darkness gathered and deepened under the trees

but he could still see the endless rain pitting the surface of the wide lake. Water trickled off his chin. The paddle was slippery in his wet hands. As it got colder, his fingers and toes grew numb. Lance shivered in the bow.

The shore was lost in misty darkness as Don toiled into the home lake. He peered anxiously ahead, wiping the rain from his eyes with the back of his hand. There it was, a light on the dock! Tired as he was, he could almost have burst into cheers. Lance whimpered eagerly. The last mile was as hard on Don's muscles as any of the others but his spirits soared, even though the rain still came down in sheets as he approached the little dock with its glimmering light. A hundred yards out, Lance raised his head and yelped a greeting.

A square of yellow light showed as the door opened, and his father dashed down to the landing with a flashlight in his hand. The beam glistened on his wet oilskins as he leaned over the edge of the dock, calling to Don. "Hello there! Did you find anyone? I heard the plane down there before the rain started."

After Lance leaped ashore, Don climbed stiffly out of the canoe. "Got them aboard all right." He straightened his back carefully. "They were banged up a lot but nothing serious, I guess."

"Go on in and get dry," urged his father. "I'll beach the canoe."

Don trudged up the familiar path. At the door his mother greeted him with open arms. "Get right out of those wet clothes. I have some hot soup for you," she said happily.

Lance, who had been shaking himself vigorously, thrust between them into the bright warmth of the kitchen. He padded into the living room and sprawled before the open fire without a word of rebuke from Mrs. Murray.

She handed Don two warm towels from the stove and urged him toward his room. "Everything's ready to eat so don't be too long."

Don dropped his clothes in a soggy heap on the floor and rubbed himself with the rough warm towels. Dry clothes were almost as good as a rest. When he returned to the living room and saw Lance sprawled before the fire, Don felt like singing. The dog's wet fur steamed a little in the warmth; he stretched his head along the floor to look up at Don, and his tail thumped lazily. Not even the hot soup was a more welcome sight.

Don felt vigour flow back into him as he ate. When his hunger was satisfied, he described the trip and Lance's part in the rescue. The wolf dog stopped pushing his empty food plate round to sit beside Don and stare up into his face. Soon the dog gave a great yawn and a moment later Don did the same.

His father laughed. "Looks as though yawns are catching!"

"They both have good reason to yawn," said his mother. "Now you get right to bed, Donald, and tell us the rest of it to-morrow."

Lance followed Don into his bedroom and stretched out on the floor to watch him. Later, in the darkness, the last sound Don heard was the wolf dog's gusty sigh as he settled himself to sleep on the rug beside the bed, willing at last to accept the shelter of the house.

10. HOME AGAIN

LIFE at the camp slipped back into the normal routine. On his next trip in to the mine, Don learned that the bush pilot had got Hayes and Cushing safely to a hospital at Lake Saint John. Hayes remained there with a bad siege of pneumonia, but Cushing wrote his thanks a few days later from New York.

Out at the lake the days were getting cooler, and at night the heat of both stove and fireplace were necessary to keep out the chill that was drifting down from the north.

Lance no longer had any fear of living and sleeping indoors. He would lie and doze before the roaring fire so close that it seemed he must be roasted by the heat. He would have been just as comfortable sleeping outside where a chill wind whipped in off the lake, while a lacy bordering of ice formed in sheltered spots where the water was still. His savage ancestry and his wild upbringing had made him indifferent to extremes of temperature.

Each morning Don sadly checked off on the calendar the days that remained of their stay at the lakeside cabin. It was too cool to swim, but he still loved to paddle around the lake or tramp through the woods that bordered it. Fishing was still good, and he and Lance warred intermittently on the red squirrels as they gathered their stores for the winter.

One brisk blue morning, some men from the mine came to help haul the canoe dock out of the water and store it for the winter. Roofs and shutters were checked and tightened. They heaped earth around the cabin to keep out driven snow during the storms ahead. Finally the two canoes were hauled out of the water and put away.

Lance watched with some alarm the work that changed the place where he had lived all summer. He sensed the coming departure and he never let Don out of his sight, day or night. If he lost him for five minutes, he prowled restlessly around until he found him again.

Don began to realize that getting Lance home would not be as much of a problem as he had feared. During the pleasant weeks of summer, he and the big wolf dog had become real friends, not to be separated by any momentary fright or sudden panic.

When the final day of holiday came and Mr. Murray shuttered the windows and locked the door from the outside, Lance felt as downcast as his master, and looked it. But there was no hesitation in the way he tramped down the trail to the mine with Don. And somewhere about halfway to the air strip, when Don began to cheer up at the thought of the friends and the activities that were awaiting him at home, Lance seemed to cheer up, too. Before long he was chasing squirrels with carefree abandon.

The trip from the mine was made in a big DC-3, and Lance climbed in without hesitation when he saw Don swing up into the plane. He watched all the family carefully as they settled down for the trip, but most of the time his eyes were on his master. The boy's confidence strengthened him to endure the unusual sounds and swayings of the take-off. Soon after they were in the air, he fell asleep at Don's feet.

At the big border airport the family changed to a small company plane and Lance was a little more nervous. The crowds of people, the massed cars, and the sounds of planes warming up in hangars and on the wide field—all were new and frightening. He pressed close to Don's knee and looked up often for reassurance.

The weather was warmer here, and the pilot of the smaller plane told them there was a real September heat wave waiting for them down in the city.

"Just the opposite of our trip last spring, remember?" sighed Don. "I wish I could have stayed up at camp until school opened."

"I have to get all your clothes ready," answered his

mother, "and I wasn't going to leave you alone up there again. You'd probably have a pet moose the next time I saw you."

The plane droned on through afternoon and sunset into darkness. The lights of a little city were a warm blur ahead when the pilot spoke briefly into his radio and the plane tilted forward in a gradual descent.

Far below them a pattern of lights sprang into the lines of a runway, and the plane swung away from them into the landing pattern. Cool scents of woods and meadows drifted up as they circled slowly over the darkness and back toward the lighted field. Suddenly the ground was under them and they seemed to be going very much faster. The wheels touched and the plane bumped and slowed to a stop.

The little airport was almost deserted, but Judy and the friends she had been visiting came hurrying over in a group. There was a happy flurry of greetings. The familiar faces were good to see. Jitters danced around, yelping excitedly, and Lance moved slowly back from the little crowd. He seemed reserved and distant but his tail swung slowly from side to side.

Jimmy Russo sought out Don while their sisters and parents chatted happily.

"Lance, this is Jimmy," said Don, as he patted the dog's shoulder. "He lives next door to us, so you're going to see a lot of him."

Jimmy had a hundred questions to ask about the big

dog and Don was only too happy to boast of his pet's adventures and his own. Finally his father interrupted. "Come on, son. The Russos have been waiting supper for us. Let's not hold them up any longer."

They piled into two cars, still busily talking. Fifteen minutes later they were grouped around the Russos' big dining-room table.

"I ought to run over and start house cleaning right away," said Mrs. Murray, "but it's so nice to relax after a trip."

"Judy and I aired your place to-day," said Mrs. Russo, passing dishes around the table. "But we've had sneak thieves in the neighbourhood, so we didn't open the downstairs windows at all."

They sat at the table for a long time after dinner, talking of their holidays and of the opening of school, until Judy gave a wide yawn, which she smothered politely.

"It's time for bed," announced Mrs. Murray, standing up, and there was no protest from Don or Judy.

They trailed across the back yard, thanking the Russos and calling their good nights as they waded through the damp grass.

"Look at that dust!" exclaimed Mrs. Murray as she snapped on the kitchen light. "Judy, you'll have to help me to-morrow morning the very first thing."

"Let's not even look at it to-night," said Judy. "I'm tired."

Mr. Murray snapped the catch on the kitchen door. "Did you see how deep that grass is, Don?" he said. "You'll have to get after it to-morrow."

"Come on, Lance," sighed Don. "We're going to need our rest."

11. LANCE AND THE POLICE

THE lights in the Murray home had been out for half an hour when a battered old car turned into the street. The driver threw it out of gear and coasted the last hundred yards to a silent stop in the shadow of a tall elm tree. He switched off the ignition and looked carefully around.

"This is it, Mike," he said softly to his companion. "That house next door with the lights upstairs belongs to people named Russo. They usually turn in about now."

"You're sure nobody's home, Joe?" asked the other man.

"I came by an hour ago and turned the car around here. My lights went right across the front of the house and all the windows were closed."

Mike reached under the dashboard and brought out a revolver. He took a flashlight from the glove compartment.

"Use matches first until you're sure the blinds are all down," warned Joe.

At that moment a porch light halfway down the block was turned on.

"Hold it!" said Mike.

They watched while a departing couple came out on the porch and talked for several minutes with their hosts. Finally they strolled down to their car and got in it.

"Down!" warned Joe as the headlights came on.

They ducked low until the car had passed and the porch light was turned off. A moment later the lights in the Russo home winked out.

"O.K.!" said Mike. "Now one more check. If a police car comes along, you've flooded your carburettor. If they get nosey, run your starter with the key off and I'll lay low for a while."

"Right!" said Joe. "If things really look bad, I'll get started and race my motor. That means I'll pick you up one block over."

"Yeah, that's it!" agreed Mike. "But don't go unless you have to. We won't get another chance here because these people are due back any day now. Take it easy, kid."

He slipped out of the car and closed the door softly behind him. He walked on the grass beside the pavement as far as the entrance to the Murray house and turned in there. He checked the downstairs windows again in the light of a distant street lamp. They were all closed and the blinds were drawn. The upstairs windows were deep in the tree shadow.

He circled the house on the side away from the Russos until he came to a sloping cellar door, which led up to a window. He tested the boards carefully before creeping up them. He slipped a short jemmy under the lower sash of the window and pressed down slowly. There was a soft splintering sound and a crack as the latch gave way. He raised the window, stepped inside, and closed the window behind him. A lighted match carefully shielded in his hand revealed the dining room. He ran a finger tip across the table and it came up black with dust.

He dropped the match on the floor and crossed to an open archway. Another lighted match showed the living room with one blind halfway up on the Russos' side of the house. He blew out the match and tiptoed over to pull the blind down. Only then did he feel safe to snap on his flashlight and look around more carefully. Silverware would be down here, he thought. He would take care of that and then look upstairs for jewellery and clothes.

Upstairs Lance lay wide awake at the foot of Don's bed. There were so many unusual sounds that he could not sleep. He listened carefully and wondered about the man who was walking around downstairs. It was hard to know whether or not that was all right. This was a strange new world and Lance did not understand it yet.

He got quietly to his feet and walked to the head of the stairs. He listened for several minutes in some doubt. Then he went back to Don's room. He had reached a decision. Don slept soundly with only a sheet covering him; Lance took the edge of the sheet carefully in his teeth and pulled. It slid smoothly off on the floor.

Don muttered softly to himself and reached out; there was nothing there. He rolled over and groped on the floor. Lance took the boy's pyjama sleeve in his teeth and tugged gently. Half awake, Don sat up and tried to pull his arm free, but Lance hung on without a sound.

"Lie down, Lance!" Don ordered in a soft whisper.

The dog would not be shaken loose; he tugged gently but steadily. Don got drowsily to his feet and tried to pull his sleeve from the insistent grip. Finally he unbuttoned the pyjama top and let it slip off. He was sleepily trying to crawl back into bed when Lance dropped the sleeve and took another grip on one of the pyjama legs. He tugged firmly several times.

That finally brought Don to his senses. He patted the dog. "What's the matter, boy?" he whispered. "Show me!"

Lance padded to the open door and looked back expectantly. Don followed him, his bare feet moving soundlessly over the rugs. At the head of the stairway, Lance stood with erect ears and quivering nose. He cocked his head on one side and then the other before he looked inquiringly up at Don.

The boy stared down into the darkness. He felt a sudden chill of excitement as a pencil of light wavered momentarily across the polished floor. Then he heard the soft chink of silverware.

"Stay, Lance!" whispered Don and pointed to the floor.

Seconds later he laid his hand gently on his father's mouth. Mr. Murray's steady breathing changed to a stifled gasp of surprise.

"Somebody's downstairs, Dad!" Don whispered. "I think it's a burglar. Lance woke me up."

"Don't go down there!" warned his father, groping for the bedside phone. "I'll dial Operator and ask for a radio car."

Picking up one of his father's shoes, Don slipped out of the room as the telephone dial clicked rapidly.

Lance was still gazing anxiously downstairs, but there was no sound from below. Then a tiny pool of light moved into the living room through the archway. Only the stranger's shoes were visible. He seemed to be listening, for he paused without a sound.

Unable to stand the suspense, Don spoke, his voice shrill with excitement. "Don't move or I'll shoot!" he cried, hurling the shoe at the flashlight.

The next instant came the flash and crack of a revolver shot, and plaster stung Don's face as a bullet slapped into the wall beside his head. Lance flung himself forward into the blackness with a growl that sounded like a roar.

Mr. Murray plunged out into the hall and flipped on the downstairs light switch. "Are you hurt, son?" he demanded, and at the same moment Judy and her mother began to scream wildly.

Don caught a glimpse of the revolver and the flashlight skating different ways across the floor as the burglar shrieked in pain.

"Come on, Dad!" He plunged down the stairs.

Lance had thrown the man to the floor with a grip on his shoulder and was tugging at him fiercely. The man punched wildly at him with his free arm, leaving his throat unguarded for an instant. Lance drove in for that vulnerable spot and the man's frightened scream was suddenly cut off.

Outside the banshee wail of a siren sounded. Mr. Murray dashed over to open the door for the policeman.

Don pulled Lance away from the silent, motionless man on the floor, frightened at the speed and fury of his attack and the fierce effectiveness of his jaws.

"What's going on here?" demanded the policeman as he charged through the door. "Oh, hello, Mr. Murray," he said more quietly. Then he saw the still figure of the burglar with blood on his throat. "What's the matter? Have an accident?"

"No. It's no accident. This burglar fired on Don when he surprised him and the dog took things over."

"Whew-w-w!" whistled the policeman. "This is a job for Stan, my partner; he's the first-aid expert. We'll send for an ambulance." He went to the door and called out to his friend in the police car. "Bring the aid kit!"

When Stan came in, he was pushing a reluctant stranger ahead of him. "Guess who I met outside," he said, smiling. "Joe Smith! Said he was waiting for a trolley bus. Had no idea his old friend Mike was any-where in the neighbourhood." He gave the newcomer a shake. "Stand over there, Joe!" he said sternly. "And don't move."

Stan knelt beside the burglar and began swabbing gently at his lacerated throat and shoulder. "Hand me those scissors, will you, Mac?" he said. "I'll have to cut this shirt off."

As the two policemen leaned over the prisoner, Joe thought he saw a chance for escape. He took two swift, silent steps toward the door. Lance rose to his feet, eyes narrowed and ruff bristling in silent menace. The man moved quickly back to his place and shrank against the wall.

From the head of the stairs, Judy and Mrs. Murray peered down.

"You'd better go back to bed," Mr. Murray advised them. "I don't think you'd like to see this fellow right now."

Lance watched quietly, as a man in a white coat entered and helped first to place the battered burglar on a stretcher and then carry him out to a long white car that stood in the street with its motor throbbing quietly.

The dog stood on the porch beside Don while the blanket-wrapped figure was slid into the ambulance.

That was the moment that Joe Smith had been waiting for. Keeping his eye on Lance, he slipped over to the end of the porch and dropped to the ground. When Lance saw him, he was running silently across the next lawn.

Lance growled and nudged Don's leg. The boy looked up. "Get him!" he ordered.

The wolf dog thudded down the porch with a spatter of swift steps and leaped ten feet out on the lawn. Half a dozen giant springs, and he was on the man's shoulders. With a muffled cry for help, Joe went down on his face, clasping his hands defensively over his head and neck.

"Sit, Lance!" shouted Don.

He sat, taking the command literally, on the back of the prone man, waiting proudly for the policeman who panted up a few seconds later with Don.

"I tell you, son," said Stan, when Smith had been handcuffed, "you ought to let that dog join the force. I'll guarantee he'd be a sergeant in six months. How about that Mac?"

"Six months?" grunted Mac. "Three months, no more."

During the next few days Lance became a local celebrity. A reporter and a photographer called the next morning and found Mrs. Murray in the midst of her house cleaning. They wanted to know all about Lance. They snapped pictures of him alone, with Don, and later with the two radio patrolmen.

After the story was published, members of the police force came one after the other to the house for a look at the renowned dog. Lance liked these big red-faced men in blue uniforms who never bothered him with patting or cooing. They just looked at him, murmured a deep-voiced "Good boy!" or "Fine fella!" and went quietly away. Mr. Murray was surprised to receive a letter which enclosed a card of honorary membership in the Patrolmen's Benevolent Association, made out in the name of Lance Murray.

A week later Lance's wide acquaintance on the force helped him out of an embarrassing situation. Don had taught him without any trouble at all to pick up the evening paper at the corner store. It was not a remarkable stunt, even though it involved crossing a busy street. Lance learned traffic rules easily and he had a healthy respect for the big cars and trucks that whirled along the concrete road. He realized that they were to be given the right of way.

One evening he walked down to the store with Don before the papers had come in. They waited a while, each with an ice-cream cone, but the big newspaper truck did not appear. As they crossed the street on the way home, Don pulled out his handkerchief. Neither he nor Lance noticed the big horn-handled jack-knife that slipped out and fell to the road in the middle of the busy crossing.

Ten minutes later, while Don was changing a bicycle tyre, his mother called out to him, "I see Mrs. Russo has her paper. Ours must be in, too."

Don called the dog. "Go get the paper, Lance," he ordered.

Lance raced off down the street, glad of the exercise. As he crossed the busy avenue, he saw the knife. He knew it well; he had seen Don use it a hundred times—to cut bait, to whittle sticks, to clean fish. He stopped and nosed it for a moment, but an order was an order. He had been told to get the paper. He looked up to see if the way was clear and crossed over to the stationery shop.

The proprietor saw him waiting with alert ears before the counter and reached behind him for the Murrays' paper. He folded it and handed it down. Lance strolled proudly out and started to cross the street.

There lay the knife. He paused, undecided what to do. He had the newspaper and he couldn't carry both. He stood for several minutes and then placed the paper beside the knife and sat down in the middle of the street. Don would come and straighten things out, he was sure.

Half a dozen cars passed by on either side. A bus driver tooted at him. A boy on a bicycle hailed him by name. Finally an elderly gentleman drove slowly past in a large car with a stout lady beside him on the front seat.

"Look at that silly dog lying in the street!" she announced. "Chauncey, stop here and chase him back on the pavement."

"Yes, m'dear," answered Chauncey and swung the car in to the kerb.

He turned off the ignition and walked back to a point opposite Lance. "Here, boy! Here, boy!" he called.

Lance looked up and swung his tail agreeably but did not move.

Chauncey looked back at his wife and spread his hands helplessly. She waved him imperiously out into the street. He looked carefully up and down and then walked out to Lance. "Come, boy!" he coaxed. "Get out of the street."

Lance looked up amiably and stayed where he was.

Chauncey peered down through his glasses and saw the knife and the newspaper. "Upon my word!" he exclaimed, and reached for them.

A growl like a distant rumble of thunder vibrated far down in Lance's throat, and the man snatched back his hand as though he had touched a hot iron.

His wife had climbed out of the car and was watching from the pavement. "What's the matter, Chauncey?" she inquired sharply.

"He won't move," explained her husband. "He seems to be guarding something."

"Bring it here, whatever it is, and let him guard it on the sidewalk," she ordered.

"He won't let me!"

"Nonsense!" she declared. "I'll take it away from him."

She marched boldly out into the street as though she were leading a parade. She stared down at the dog and reached for the newspaper.

In the flick of an eyelash, Lance was on his feet, glaring. He snarled ferociously, with his lips drawn back and his eyes narrowed to slits, and seized the newspaper.

The lady had courage. She reached for the jack-knife. Lance shifted his attention in a flash. He dropped the paper and growled fiercely with his nose an inch away from the knife.

"The dog is mad!" announced the lady positively. "We must get a policeman. I think we passed one at the last corner. Come, Chauncey." They walked back to the corner.

Constable Stern, on point duty, was startled by the lady's imperious call. He mopped his sweating brow and walked over. "Yes, ma'am?" he inquired politely.

"There's a mad dog down the street and I want you to shoot him," she announced firmly.

The patrolman walked down the street with her. "You know we don't shoot mad dogs any more, unless we have to," he explained politely. "The veterinaries say. . . ." He never finished the sentence.

"When I was a girl, policemen shot them on sight," she informed him.

The patrolman looked at her and thought what a long

time ago that was, but wisely refrained from saying so.

"There's the dog now," she said, pointing at Lance. "He almost bit me."

"Why, that's Don Murray's dog," exclaimed the officer.

"And who might Don Murray be?" inquired the lady sarcastically. "Is he the mayor of this town?"

"Don't you know him, lady?" asked Stern in surprise. "Why, he owns this dog. I guarded Mike Williams in the hospital after he tried to rob the Murray house, and I saw what that dog did to him. I wouldn't touch that paper if it was a package of thousand-dollar bills."

"Well, what are you going to do? The dog is obstructing traffic."

"Just a minute, lady." Officer Stern walked over to the dark-green call box on the corner telephone pole. He spoke briefly into the little mouthpiece.

Half a minute later a radio car eased to a stop in front of the Murray home and the siren gave a brief wail.

"Hey, Don," called the driver to the boy, who was working in front of the garage. "Come on and take a ride."

Don hurried down to the kerb and the two grinning policemen explained Officer Stern's predicament. The boy got into the back seat and the car whirled off down the street. A moment later they drew up before the group composed of Stern, Chauncey, and his wife. Don opened the door and hopped out.

Lance thumped his tail in welcome. He had known his master would come. Don picked up the knife and the dog picked up the paper.

"Gee, thanks!" said Don. "That certainly was nice of you fellows."

"It's the least we could do for a PBA member," said the driver as he slipped the car into gear.

Officer Stern went back to his post with a smile.

The large lady climbed grimly into the car beside her husband. "Petty politics is the curse of this country, Chauncey," she exclaimed. "Drive on!"

"Yes, m'dear," said Chauncey, and drove on.

12. LANCE TAKES UP FARMING

THE next evening at the supper table Mr. Murray raised his eyebrows in surprise at an item in the evening paper. "Did you see this, Mother?" He read it aloud.

"Noted P.B.A. Member Blocks Traffic on North Avenue. Dog Guards Property on Busy Street.

"It took the combined efforts of three policemen, a radio car, several interested citizens, and Donald Murray, Jr., of Cedar Street to remove Lance, a German Shepherd dog, from his post amid rush-hour traffic on North Avenue late yesterday afternoon. Lance was guarding valuable property belonging to young Murray. This consisted of a large jack-knife and a copy of the *Meadowville Mirror*."

Mr. Murray folded the paper and slapped it down at his side. "There's more of it," he said, frowning at Don, "but that gives you the general idea. Is this sort of thing going to continue indefinitely?"

Don grinned, and mumbled something through a mouthful of potatoes.

"When does school open?" asked his father.

"A week from Monday," he answered, with regret in his voice.

"Well, if this sort of thing keeps up, we'll have a stream of people coming around here to get Lance's autograph," said Mr. Murray. "I think you ought to get out of town for a while. I had a letter from Uncle Tim the other day. How would you like to run up to Vermont and visit him for a week?"

"Hey, that would be great! Can Jimmy Russo go?"

"It's a good idea," said Mrs. Murray. "I could drive up with you and stay overnight. I've been wanting to see Aunt Bridget."

They phoned Uncle Tim that night, and early the next morning Jimmy and Don and his mother, together with Lance and Jitters, piled into the car for the trip. Up the highway and over the Pulaski Skyway and through the Holland Tunnel, the boys watched Lance's reactions to the crowded and unusual scenes. His ears were erect and his head swivelled from side to side as he tried to see everything. They had brought Jitters along to reassure him, but the small dog promptly curled up and went to sleep. Driving was an old story to him.

When they reached the long stretches of parkway, Lance leaned far out of the window, sniffing the breeze and staring at the fields and patches of woodland. Occa-

F

sional woodchucks sat up on their hind legs to watch the car pass. Lance stared back at them and whimpered excitedly as though he would like to chase them back to their burrows. Even Jitters roused himself to yap at them.

The party ate lunch in the car at the side of the road and hurried on. By mid-afternoon they had turned off the concrete on to a narrow dirt road that led up into the hills. At the top of a rise they saw the low white house and huge red barn that marked Uncle Tim's place.

He was waiting on the porch with Aunt Bridget to greet them. Jitters and Lance were met by Shep, the stately old collie. Jitters leaped all over the big fellow, yapping and licking his face, while Lance walked up to him in a more dignified manner. A slow circling and sniffing of noses followed, and by the time Don and Jimmy had escaped from the porch the dogs were friends.

The boys, accompanied by the dogs, headed for the barnyard to explore the scenes familiar to all except Lance. They visited the pigs, the horses, the chickens, and the little flock of long-necked, suspicious geese that gabbled and hissed at them ill-naturedly. The mows were crammed with hay, and Jimmy and Don took a few leaps into the fragrant mounds from a high beam, with the dogs watching curiously from the floor below.

When milking time came, some of the cows were already waiting at the pasture bars. They crowded in when Uncle Tim took down the long poles that formed the gate, and pushed their way to their places in the stanchions.

Uncle Tim ran a practised eye over them. "Some of 'em are still down in the swamp," he said. "Go get 'em, Shep. Can that dog of yours help, Don?"

"He's a smart dog," said Don, "but he never saw cows close up before."

"German Shepherd, ain't he?" asked Uncle Tim. "If he can herd sheep, I guess he can herd cows too."

Lance dashed off through the field behind Shep. Five minutes later, he came proudly back, ranging with watchful care behind the little bunch of cattle.

At supper that night Uncle Tim praised Lance. "Glad to have a dog like that around the place these days," he said, helping himself to baked beans. "Those wild dogs from upcountry have been around lately."

"Wild dogs?" asked Jimmy, pouring ketchup on his beans.

"Eight or ten of them, they say," explained Ted, the hired man. "Never saw them myself, but I've heard them up on the mountain moonlight nights."

"Ayuh! They've been running deer all summer," said Uncle Tim. "They got together last winter when the snow was deep. They killed an awful lot of deer."

"Where'd they come from?" inquired Don.

"Some are runaways and some are born wild, I guess," his uncle explained. "And some could be dogs that sneak away from home nights for a taste of venison."

"Would they bother cattle?" asked Jimmy, digging into the beans again.

"They pulled down a heifer over beyond the river last week," said Ted with a frown.

"I wish I'd brought my .22 along," sighed Don.

"If you want to try and shoot a wild dog, you go right in and take one of my guns," his uncle offered. He went on to expound his favourite theory. "Every gun on my place is loaded; they're safer that way. It's the empty guns that kill people."

On Sunday afternoon, all the people at the farm drove to the village to help with the work on the new Grange Hall.

"It's a community project," Uncle Tim explained. "We finish off with a picnic supper, so we call it a party."

There was a lot of hard work to do. Don and Jimmy loaded gravel from Uncle Tim's big gravel pit into the truck. Later they helped mix it with the cement for the Grange Hall foundation.

The farmers talked as they worked, and most of the talk was about the pack of wild dogs.

"Old Kip Southard, over the mountain, said they pulled down three of his sheep Friday night," announced one farmer. "That ought to keep them fed for a while."

"I don't know!" returned another. "Those dogs kill as much for the fun of it as for food. When dogs go bad, they're terrible mean."

"Full moon to-night, you know," pointed out a third. "That makes an awful lot of humans do foolish things. Seems like it can affect dumb animals, too."

Several men were ready to agree to that.

"It was the time of the full moon in July when they raided that chicken farm over to the Corners," one of them recalled. "Fellow shot two of them that night but he must have lost a hundred hens, pretty near."

"I see you've got a new dog down at your place, Tim," commented a tall wiry farmer by the name of Tom Wallace.

"That's a fine dog, too, Tom," admitted Uncle Tim. "Belongs to my nephew here." He patted Don on the shoulder.

"You keep an eye on that dog, son!" said Wallace with a frown. "If he gets to running nights, he might go bad. I never did trust those p'lice dogs."

"Lance go bad?" Don laughed. "Why, I'd trust him anywhere."

"Well, just don't you trust him near my sheep. That's a mighty valuable flock I've got up next to your place, and I aim to keep it."

Don didn't say anything more. He noticed that everyone took the wild dogs very seriously, and he could understand why. The safety of their stock and their farm animals meant their living.

The busy afternoon slipped quietly into evening almost before anyone noticed. The women at the picnic tables called again and again for the men to come to supper, but they were reluctant to waste any of the daylight. The sun was well down below the horizon when they finally washed off their shovels and covered the foundation against possible rain.

They ate as heartily as they had worked; the moon was climbing over the distant hills like a huge orange balloon before the last of the food was cleaned up. The men gathered in little groups with pipes and mugs of coffee to discuss politics. Children from Junior Grange and Four-H were singing songs. Another little crowd around a car radio listened to the late baseball scores.

"Sunday is a day of rest," said Uncle Tim, stretching. "But I'm always late getting around to it."

13. DEATH IN THE MOONLIGHT

AT the farm Lance watched the same orange moon as it slipped upward above the black outline of the mountain. Memories of other moons and other scenes stirred his wolf blood. He longed to sit back on his haunches, raise his muzzle to the sky, and howl, as thousands of his ancestors had done for centuries. The yearning quivered out in his throat as a vague whimper. He was a dog now, and he had duties to think about.

He trotted out to circle the barn and listen to the sounds of life inside. One of the horses thudded a restless hoof against the flooring of his stall; a hen roosting on a rafter clucked sleepily and stirred in the darkness. There was a subdued squeaking of mice from the haymow. Everything seemed to be all right, but Lance felt an unusual restlessness. He walked back to the shed where Jitters and Shep sprawled asleep on a bedding of burlap grain bags. He lay down beside them with his head on

167

his outstretched paws and watched the moon as it climbed higher into the cloudless sky.

His restlessness grew stronger. He raised his head and sniffed the light breeze, his nose rising with each breath. His alert ears moved to catch the tiniest sound. Gradually the vague uneasiness gave way to a sure sense of danger. At first there was just the slight bristling of his ruff as he grew aware of some unknown peril. Then all at once his ears and nose warned him unmistakably that a hunting pack was on the prowl somewhere near him.

He did not feel the slightest desire to join such a pack, although six months before he would have dashed gladly to meet them. His training and his devotion to Don had changed him. Now he felt only a fierce loyalty to the ground on which he stood and a determination to defend the farm and its animals.

He was on his feet now and prowling back and forth before the shed, a silent guardian shadow. The other two dogs, who did not have his wolf-keen scent and hearing and that sharp sixth sense that was the product of his wild ancestry, slept on, oblivious to the danger.

Lance knew that less than half a mile away a pack of wild dogs was stealing softly through the brush toward the sheep he had seen that very morning. It aroused his anger. If he had been warned to guard the sheep, he would even now have been rocketing through the darkness to defend them; but they were not his. All that stirred his anger was the near presence of this threat to his farm and his cows. He patrolled the barnyard like a caged tiger, ready to defend his own.

There was a sudden distant outburst of wild howls and yelps, a demon hunting chorus. The two sleeping dogs were awake and on their feet in an instant. The fierce baying lasted less than a minute and then there was a hush as sudden as the outbreak. Lance knew that the pack had fallen upon its prey. There was a single frantic cry from a dying sheep, followed by complete silence. The pack was feeding now.

Jitters whined and whimpered; he knew only that somewhere near were dogs, hunting and having fun. He wanted to join them, but a vague feeling that he should remain where he had been placed on guard restrained him.

Lance growled a warning to him as he wandered, complaining, toward the end of the yard. It was no use; some sudden scent on the wind decided him. With a yelp of eagerness he slipped through the fence and went barking off across the fields to the scene of action.

The big dog stared angrily after him and growled his disgust. He stood with cocked ears and alert nose following the spaniel's progress across the moonlit fields. He was out of sight almost instantly in the heavy grass, but Lance knew of his whereabouts almost as though he had been watching a television screen in his sensitive brain.

The little dog broke into the open a hundred yards

from the spot where the pack was worrying the carcasses of three dead sheep. That was all that saved him. This tiny intruder could not have stood up to the smallest of the hard-bitten outlaws and he looked like safe game to them. They abandoned their kill and dashed for him with yelps of pleasure.

Jitters swerved as he saw the pack rushing for him. He realized on the instant that he was in mortal danger. The safety of the barnyard was a long quarter mile away; he could never hope to reach it. There was a pile of dried brush in the nearest corner of the sheep pasture and he raced for it with all his speed. Behind him the pack scented his fear on the wind and howled their delight. The first of them was barely a stride behind Jitters and closing fast when the little fellow scuttled into the brush like a homing woodchuck.

In the barnyard Lance followed the progress of the discovery and chase by the tone of the dogs' outcries. He did not know of the brush pile, but he could tell that Jitters had reached some kind of temporary safety by the sound of the pack's yelps. He knew that his small companion was in great danger but still fighting, for he could distinguish his shrill valiant voice in the general chorus. Jitters had taken refuge under a heavy branch in the pile and nipped the nose of a huge dog who had reached in to snap at him.

The renegades surrounded the pile. This was better fun than the stupid sheep. They had hunted enough foxes and woodchucks and rabbits to know what to do now; they began digging under Jitters' refuge to force him out into the open.

A quarter mile away Lance was pacing the ground nervously. His duty was to stay on guard, but within earshot his small friend was being hunted to certain death. It was a fearful problem.

The stolid Shep was excited by the presence of the pack, but the danger to Jitters bothered him not a bit. The little dog was almost a stranger to him, and the farm was his home. He would stay where he was no matter what happened.

Lance finally solved his problem as a human being might have done. The danger to his friend overcame his abstract duty to the farm. A huge dog had tunnelled close enough to Jitters to snap at his shoulder, and the distant sound of that yelp of pain made up Lance's mind for him. He measured the height of the fence at a glance, took a half-dozen hasty steps, and leaped it like a deer. Across the moonlit fields in a silent burning fury he sprinted for the scene of the fight.

Not even his fierce loyalty to his friend clouded the keen cunning of his wolf mind. He slipped into the open field like a grey ghost and moved up on the encircling pack with every sense alert and tingling. He would have to strike fast and ruthlessly, for he was vastly outnumbered by the dozen dogs.

He spotted two animals as the leaders in the silent

seconds while he raced up on the unsuspecting pack. One was a huge gaunt hound with tattered ears and oddly set eyes that gave his face the appearance of a death's-head; the other was a giant mongrel with wide jaws like a steel trap and a long slanting scar between his yellow eyes. He was the one who was burrowing fiercely after the cowering Jitters.

Lance dashed forward in a fierce final sprint and leaped high over the backs of the smaller dogs in the rear. He landed as a complete surprise between the two leaders at the edge of the brush pile. Before the big hound had a chance to snap at him, Lance slashed his throat with one fierce lunge. The hound went down, kicking and dying, but the mongrel was warned by the short struggle; he whirled on the wolf dog and charged him, trying to use his greater size to knock him off his feet.

Lance dodged in the little space he had and drew back against the brush. Once down, he knew he would be overwhelmed in a matter of seconds. As the big mongrel and a smaller dog boxed him in, he growled a deep roar of rage at them, his ears flattened menacingly. They both rushed him at once like a trained team, but little Jitters was still in the fight. As the smaller of the two outlaw dogs closed in, he placed one foot in the shallow hole that had been scratched under the brush to get at Jitters. The little cocker saw his chance and seized it; he clamped his jaws on the paw and held on. The dog yelped and pulled back, leaving Lance free to meet the attack of the big yellow-eyed mongrel. He slashed his shoulder and ducked away.

At that moment a car squealed to a stop on the road bordering the pasture, and the voices of angry men were heard. As the renegade pack began drifting away into the brush, the big mongrel cast a hasty glance over his shoulder.

It was Lance's opportunity. He had a clear shot at the throat and he plunged forward. Deep through the heavy fur his teeth cut to the pulsing artery. Desperately, the bigger dog tried to tug himself away, but the wolf's slash was straight and true. When Lance released his grip, he knew with an animal's sure instinct that his enemy was dying. He slipped away into the shadows with Jitters whimpering at his side. The big mongrel staggered a dozen paces before he went down in a sprawling bloody heap.

The two men from the car had discovered the dead sheep; their voices were sharp with anger. One of them ran back to the car and swept the dim field with the beam of the auto's spotlight. The sharp white shaft swung down the line of the fence just as Lance went over it in a swift arc. The man cursed fiercely.

"It's that big police dog!" exclaimed Tom Wallace. "I told that city kid I didn't trust him."

"See him! There he goes!" called out the other man from the field. "If I had my rifle I could have knocked him right over."

"Come on, Will," growled Wallace. "I'm going home and get my gun. Then I'm going over to see Tim McGrath."

Five minutes later Uncle Tim swung into his lane from the road and stopped his car beside the dark porch. He had stayed at the Grange Hall later than he had planned.

"Put the lights on, Bridget," he said as he opened the door. "Ted and I have to get to milking right away."

"Say, it looks as though we have company," remarked Jimmy, as he climbed down from the truck a little stiffly. Ted eased the big vehicle around the parked car.

A rapidly driven car slowed down with squealing brakes and lurched into the driveway behind them. They stood there with its headlights glaring upon them until it ground to a stop.

Tom Wallace got out with his rifle under his arm and strode up to the little group. Will followed behind him with a shotgun. "Where's that police dog of yours, Tim?" he demanded harshly.

Don bristled at the tone of his voice. He stepped forward. "That's my dog. What do you want with him?"

"I'm going to shoot him," growled Wallace. "He killed three of my best Merinos to-night."

"Now wait a minute!" said Uncle Tim. "Did you see him kill your sheep?"

"I didn't have to," said Wallace angrily. "Those sheep

weren't dead more than five minutes when I drove up, and I saw your dog go over the fence when I swung my spotlight on him."

Uncle Tim turned to the hired man. "Ted, you go to milking; it's late. I'll straighten this out."

"You're not going to talk me out of anything, Tim McGrath," said Wallace bitterly. "I'm going to shoot that dog before I leave the place."

"If that dog did anything wrong, we'll destroy him ourselves," said Uncle Tim firmly. "You better leave your gun in the car. Any shooting's done on my place, I'll be the one to do it."

Mumbling angrily to himself, Wallace finally walked back to his car and set the rifle in the back seat. Will followed his example and left his shotgun.

"Hand me that flashlight, Jimmy," said Uncle Tim He led the little group toward the barnyard.

"Here, Lance!" called Don.

His anger had died away and he felt weak and sick; maybe the dog really had killed the sheep. He had probably killed wild animals for food and fun all the first year of his life. Could he be expected to change his habits in a few short months?

Lance came out of the darkness toward them, a little more slowly than usual. He was always reserved in the presence of strangers, but his hesitation looked like guilt to at least three of the little group.

Wallace flipped his light on the dog. "Look there!"

he said accusingly. "There's blood on his chest. Where did that come from, do you suppose?"

Don knelt down and called the dog closer to him. He patted his head and looked him over. Lance was still breathing heavily. The blood on his chest had not dried yet.

Uncle Tim leaned over and ran his hand through the dog's coat. "It's fresh blood, all right," he said heavily. "You might be right, Tom, but there's no need to act too hasty."

"I'm warning you, Tim McGrath," snarled Wallace. "If you let that dog get away with this, I'll have the law on you."

"Maybe he cut himself on barbed wire somewhere," suggested Jimmy, who had been watching with worried eyes as the men argued.

" 'Tain't likely!" sneered Tom Wallace.

Just then Jitters limped out of the darkness and pressed against the side of the larger dog. Lance lowered his head and licked the spaniel's wounded shoulder carefully.

"Here, boy!" called Uncle Tim, pulling the little dog toward him. He turned the light full on him. "Look!" he said. "The blood might've come from that cut."

"I tell you I saw the dog in my sheep pasture!" cried Wallace hotly.

Suddenly Don had an idea. He would put it up to Lance.

"Did you go out there, Lance?" he asked, squatting down and looking his pet full in the face.

Lance lowered his head guiltily and swung to one side, shifting his feet uneasily. Don felt cold all over.

He reminded himself that he had to face the facts. "Go ahead, Lance!" He swung his arm into the darkness. "Show us where you were!"

The dog trotted slowly off into the darkness.

"Come on," said Don. "If he leads us to the sheep, I'll believe he did it."

"I don't care what you believe," blustered Wallace, as the little group followed the reluctant dog across the dew-soaked field.

They tramped along in silence over the mown stubble. The two flashlights were unnecessary out in the open where the full moon cast a ghostly light. No one spoke until Lance approached the fence that marked the end of Uncle Tim's land. There he veered sharply to the right.

"It's over this way!" insisted Wallace.

"Shut up!" ordered Uncle Tim. "We'll follow the dog."

They made their way through the fence and looked around. Lance was a hundred feet away, nosing a shapeless dark heap in the moonlight. Beside the brush pile lay another dark form.

"Two more sheep!" cried Wallace in fierce anger. "If I had my gun I'd put an ounce of lead in him right now."

Uncle Tim plodded slowly over and turned his flashlight on the dog and his prey. He peered for a moment and then straightened up, as though a heavy weight had been removed from his shoulders.

"Sheep?" he snorted triumphantly. "Well, I guess not."

Wallace ran to his side. Don followed with a sudden breath of hope stirring in his heart.

"Humph! That don't prove nothing," growled Wallace. "Maybe they were all in it and got to fighting."

The man called Will had spotted the other dead outlaw dog.

"Say, Tom!" he called. "Here's the criminal right here. This is the one I saw last winter after those deer. He's got some of my lead in his side somewhere right now."

Don sat down on the ground and threw his arms around Lance's neck. He couldn't say a word, but he hugged the big dog and rocked him slowly back and forth.

Tom Wallace remained stubbornly silent, but Uncle Tim cleared his throat and ran his flashlight over the ground with slow care.

"Why, what kind of a woodsman are you, Tom?" he said accusingly. "Look! You can see the whole thing right here."

The tall farmer finally unbent and followed him as he pointed out the clues on the ground.

"There's some black hairs snagged on that big limb in the brush pile," Uncle Tim pointed out. "Jitters must have been cornered under there. Lance came here to drive them away."

Wallace grunted, but he looked the ground over carefully.

"Now look at the grass in the light of the beam!" Uncle Tim swung his flashlight along the ground. A wide trail showed up dark where the rush of the pack had knocked the dew from the blades of grass.

As the group trudged toward the dead sheep, the survivors pattered curiously over, bleating and staring at the beams of the flashlights.

"Look at that!" chimed in Will. "That's dog sign and lots of it. The pack was here all right."

Wallace stood alone and stubbornly silent.

Uncle Tim looked over at him. "I guess that Lance saved the rest of your flock by jumping in just when he did."

Tom Wallace heaved a big sigh. "I guess my big mouth got me in wrong again," he said. "Tim, I'm mighty sorry I shouted the way I did."

"Gosh, anybody'd feel cross if they lost three sheep like that," said Uncle Tim.

"Sure they would," said Don, patting Lance as he pressed close against his knee.

"Come on, let's get our milking done," said Uncle Tim. " 'Night, Tom."

Tom Wallace patted Don on the shoulder as he turned to go. "Don't hold it against me, son, he said quietly.

14. THE LAST OF THE PACK

MONDAY morning was crisp and cool. Uncle Tim stood at the barn door looking at the bright blue sky, while Lance and Shep drove the cows efficiently up to the gate.

"Guess we'll have nice weather for a spell," he announced, watching Lance admiringly. "We'll get some ensilage in to-day."

"We won't be able to finish it to-day, will we?" asked Jimmy.

"Oh, no!" said Uncle Tim, winking heavily at him. "We'll get right back at it to-morrow morning."

Ted almost dropped the milking machines he was carrying. "Hey, boss!" he protested in quick alarm. "To-morrow's the fair."

"The fair?" Uncle Tim looked puzzled. "Gosh, I guess I didn't count on that."

The boys laughed and Ted grinned sheepishly as he realized it was a joke.

After breakfast everyone but Ted piled into the farm truck and jounced out along a rutted track to the corn-field. They worked all morning, chopping down the green corn, piling it on the truck, and hauling it back for Ted to run into the roaring ensilage cutter. When they heard the vigorous ringing of the dinner bell through the din, they were more than ready to stop. Through the afternoon they toiled again till milking time. It was hard work and the boys were glad to turn in early that night.

Breakfast next morning was the usual extra-size affair but everyone hurried through it. Already cars from down the valley were passing the house on their way to the fair in a steady stream. Shiny new sedans and battered jalopies, noisy little jeeps and big trucks, all laden with dressed-up people, hurried by.

The boys were waiting in the car before anyone else was ready. The passing cars were fewer by the time Uncle Tim swung out into the road and headed for the highway. They were driving through a shady little village when a police siren sounded from a parked car and a tall man in grey uniform waved them to the side of the road.

"Gosh, what did you do, Uncle Tim?" asked Don, worried.

"I didn't do anything." Uncle Tim smiled placidly. "You city people always have something on your conscience."

The State trooper planted a large foot on the running board. "I've got bad news for you, Tim." He frowned.

"I just got a phone call from Elmer up in the fire lookout. He said he was looking through the glasses a few minutes ago and he saw a pack of dogs heading down the mountain toward your valley. He called a couple of farms up the road and couldn't find anybody home."

Uncle Tim pounded the steering wheel in disgust.

"Too bad it's to-day," said the trooper. "I'd go down there with you but I have to stay on traffic duty for another hour anyway. You're the first man from the valley I've seen."

"Send some more along if you see them," said Uncle Tim. "I'll get right back."

He whipped the car around and headed toward home. No one mentioned the fair. They realized that the valley was all but empty and the wild dogs could ravage at will through the unguarded farms and pastures. As they turned off the road, a car was coming out of the valley. They waved it to a stop and hailed Will and Tom Wallace.

With a grave face Uncle Tim told them of the warning sent by the fire-warden. They swung their car around and headed back into the valley behind him. The road was clear and the two cars raced on at top speed until they reached a fork in the road, where Uncle Tim stopped and the other car swung up beside him.

"We'll go home and get our rifles," said Tom Wallace. "Then we'll pick you up at your place and head up the hollow to cut them off."

"Wait a minute!" said Will. "Listen!"

A wild chorus of baying welled up across the nearest hill.

"Too late for that!" said Uncle Tim. "Come on down to my place. I've got three rifles all loaded in the kitchen."

The cars lurched forward down the road again. At the top of the next rise they caught a glimpse of the outlaw pack in full cry over the outspread fields below them.

They were not chasing sheep or cows, but Lance himself. The big wolf dog was toiling along a bare hundred feet ahead of the foremost pursuer. He must have gone out alone to meet them and draw them away from their prey.

"Hurry, Uncle Tim!" urged Don in a shaky voice. "Lance must be hurt or he'd be running faster than that."

Uncle Tim bore down harder on the accelerator and the car leaped forward. The boys stared anxiously at the progress of the chase. There were ten or eleven dogs on Lance's trail and they were spread out over nearly a hundred yards. The nearest, a long-legged rangy dog that seemed part collie, was closing rapidly with the limping wolf dog.

Suddenly they saw Lance stop dead in his tracks and whirl to face the big collie. The pursuer was going so fast that the slash Lance aimed for his throat ripped his shoulder and sent him rolling off his feet. Lance was upon him in an instant. A single clip of the jaws, and the collie lay still. Lance was off again under the noses of the pack, his long wolf stride rapidly widening the gap between them. Howling their anger, the outlaw dogs raced after him.

The men in the car shouted their encouragement, but the chase was a good quarter of a mile away across the open fields and Lance was far too busy to notice. Once again, before they reached the house, they saw him bring his wild cunning into play. The way led down a long sloping field with a wooded hollow in the centre where the ground was too swampy to plough. A thick acre-long clump of willows and sumach and tangled brush grew there.

Lance loped down the hill and past the thicket, but the moment he was hidden from the view of the pack, he cut to one side and dashed around behind the big clump of brush. The chase went streaming past and the leading dogs milled in confusion, circling and yelping when they lost the trail.

Creeping stealthily all the way around the little grove, Lance fell like a hawk upon the rear of the pack. He struck only twice. The dog at the end of the string went flying through the air as Lance grabbed him by the nape of the neck and flung him over his shoulder. The dog ahead of him turned to meet the attack and received a lightning slash at his throat that left him wriggling and kicking only a moment before he lay still.

The wolf dog was a hundred feet away in another

direction before the outlaws realized that their quarry was behind them. The diminished pack took up the chase again, yelling their fury at the elusive grey animal who had thinned their ranks with a ferocity that equalled their own.

The cars had reached the farmhouse driveway now and they swung perilously into the abrupt curve. Ted threw open the door of the sedan before it stopped, and leaped nimbly out as it slid to a halt. His feet pounded briefly on the porch as he sped to the unlocked kitchen. A moment later he was back with the rifles cradled in his arms and a box of shells bulging his coat pocket. He handed rifles out to Uncle Tim and Tom Wallace, keeping one himself.

"Here, Will, you're a better shot than I am," offered Uncle Tim.

"No. Keep it, and I'll drive my car. It's faster."

They piled into the second car, gravel churning up behind it as it leaped into motion.

The dogs were across the road now and seemed to be heading back the way they had come on the trail of the elusive Lance. The men had only the wind-blown sound of baying to guide them, and the car raced on down the road with everyone straining for a sight of the pack.

"I counted seven left on their feet," said Don. "If we can only cut down a few more, maybe Lance'll be able to finish them."

As they topped a little hill, they came into view of the

running dogs again. Lance was far ahead, with the remaining pursuers trailing in a long string behind him. The nearest of the wild dogs was three hundred yards away from the road, across the rolling fields.

"Stop! We'll get a shot from here," said Ted.

The second crop of clover had been cut from the fields only a week or two before and the ground was as clear as a lawn.

"Wait a minute!" said Don. "I think he's going to hit them again!"

Lance has taken a hasty glance over his shoulder as he raced across the brow of a little ridge in the midst of the open fields. The moment he was hidden from the pack by the rise, he turned sharply to one side and dropped to the ground, watching the summit of the hill. The leader of the hunt shot over the rim at full speed and broke into excited yelping at the sight of the prey so near at hand. His momentum carried him on past in a wide curve as he struggled to turn.

Lance ignored him; he rose to a half crouch and slipped forward with his belly almost on the ground. His tail twitched restlessly as he neared the point where the next dog would appear. His timing was perfect. He broke into a slouching run and then dashed forward just as the second dog tore unsuspectingly over the crest. Lance bowled him over on his back with the weight of his charge and straddled his body to deliver a flurry of snaps and slashes that broke through the guard of the dog's bared teeth. In an instant, Lance was galloping off at full speed in a new direction and the fallen dog was kicking feebly on his back in a last reflex.

"That leaves only six," exulted Don.

The car had stopped on the road and Ted leaped out with his rifle at the ready. He levelled it and sighted the end dog of the pack as he slowed down to turn. It seemed a long time as Ted's finger tightened slowly on the trigger. His target was the only dog left in sight when the sharp crack of the shot rang out.

There was a puff of dust a few feet from the side of the running dog. He made a complete somersault and lay still. He never stirred again.

"Good shooting!" said Jimmy.

"Lucky!" Ted frowned. "The ricochet got him, or I'd have missed him clean."

"That's five," said Will. "Come on! There's a barway into the next field."

Ted got back into the car, and they raced down the road a quarter of a mile. Tom Wallace leaped out to swing the wide gate open, and the car bumped and bounced through.

"Watch your springs!" warned Uncle Tim, as the car picked up speed and careened wildly across the rough ground.

"Heck with my springs!" retorted Will. "It's worth a busted spring to watch that Lance dog operate."

They did not get a glimpse of the chase again until

they had driven to the top of the rising ground at the end of the field. It was a high point with a wide view of the valley below.

"He's heading for the gravel pit," said Uncle Tim. "Look there! He's circling back now."

"He was there on Sunday with us," said Jimmy. "I bet he remembered it."

They piled out of the car and wriggled through the fence that barred the way. A hundred yards ahead was the crumbling edge of the great gravel pit. They waded toward it through bushes and scrub growth. The chase was out of sight beyond a screen of trees, but they could hear the clamour of the dogs as they drew nearer. The sound was thinner than it had been when they first heard it half an hour ago, and it did not sound as terrible as it had then.

The onlookers came out of the brush at the rim of the steep pit and far beyond it saw the little string of dogs dashing out into an open field. Lance was leading them directly toward the single entrance to the pit, opposite the place where they stood.

Ted raised his rifle and then lowered it again. "It's too risky," he said. "They're all bunched up."

Lance raced for the opening into the pit, and the five surviving dogs followed boldly, heedless of their weakened fighting strength.

"I hope Lance knows what he's doing!" Uncle Tim frowned. "We can't shoot at them down in that pit.

There's rocks all around and the ricochets would fly all ways."

"Come on! Let's get around to the entrance," urged Don. "If we get close enough, perhaps we can help him."

They began circling the steep-sided pit, stumbling and tripping as they tried to keep their eyes on the approaching chase.

Before they were half-way around, Lance reached the great excavation and shot like an arrow through the narrow entrance. Scarcely a hundred feet behind, the bunched-up outlaw dogs raced into the pit in a panting group, with lolling tongues and heaving flanks. Only one of the five was anywhere near the size of Lance.

"Look!" said Wallace. "More cars are coming up." Along the dusty road that led to the gravel pit, three cars were speeding toward the entrance. Farther back two more were coming into sight over a rise in the ground.

Down in the pit, Lance's strategy became clear. He tore across its uneven floor to the farthest side; then he wheeled abruptly, like a half-back reversing his field. Back he raced like an avenging fury, slashing and snarling as he dodged through the ranks of his pursuers. They were taken completely by surprise at the sudden fierceness of his attack. Before they realized his purpose, he was back at the entrance, standing guard over it with bared teeth.

One of the renegade dogs lay kicking and struggling

in his last agony; another circled, yelping, on three legs. The tables were completely turned. The pursuing pack had been reduced to three effective fighters and, instead of chasing a fleeing foe, they were bottled up in a complete trap.

The men on the rim of the pit broke into a run to reach the entrance and back up Lance. One of the dogs, more far-sighted than the rest, realized his position and turned back. He dashed to one of the sloping sides and began a frantic effort to climb the sandy wall that crumbled and slid beneath his feet.

"There's a safe shot," said Ted. He aimed, sighted, and squeezed off a shot. The climbing dog collapsed and rolled to the bottom of the pit. He lay crumpled and still, with the sand sifting down on him.

"Only two left!" cried Don. "Go get 'em, Lance!"

As the men slid and jumped down at the side of the entrance, the wolf dog realized that his long struggle was at an end. He leaped forward, and the two dogs facing him separated at the fury of his attack. He ran one down in four strides and tore his throat out as he passed. The other dog fled to the farthest end of the pit and Uncle Tim finished him with a single shot while Tom Wallace put the wounded dog out of his misery with a bullet in the head.

The long chase ended as quickly as that. The men walked quietly back to the mouth of the gravel pit. Lance, in spite of his fatigue and a long deep slash on one shoulder, padded stiffly over to each dog in turn to sniff and examine him.

"Better stay away from him a while, Don," warned his uncle. "He'll need some time to calm down."

Don ignored his advice and walked quietly forward. He sat down alone on the ground and began talking softly to the big wolf dog. Lance turned away from the slain dogs and swung his tail slowly to and fro. He limped over to his master and rubbed his uninjured shoulder against the boy's knees. Then he curled up beside him and began to lick and cleanse the long wound on his shoulder where the teeth of one of the dogs had cut deeply.

The occupants of the other cars had arrived in the meantime. Don looked up to see Uncle Tim standing beside him with a big, calm-looking young man. "This is Dr. Steel, the vet from town," he said. "He thought we might need him down here when he heard about the wild dogs."

"Yes," said the veterinarian in his deep slow voice. "I'm glad to see there's only one patient to treat instead of a dozen or two. Don't you think we'd better take Lance back to my place in town? If I put a few stitches in that cut, it may not even leave a scar."

"Won't it hurt him?" asked Don anxiously.

"I don't think so," said the vet. "I'll give him a local anaesthetic first. When we get through with him, he'll be as good as new."

"All right," said Don. "We'll be right with you."

An hour later, at the vet's office, when they finally slipped the muzzle off Lance's nose, he sniffed at Don and licked his hand.

The boy seemed more shaken by the treatment than his dog. He looked out through the open door at the men waiting on the grass. "You go ahead to the fair," he said. "I'll stay here with Lance for a while."

"I'll wait for you," said Uncle Tim. "The rest can go on with the Wallaces."

"Sure they can!" agreed Tom Wallace. "We'll get right along, now that Lance is all right. But bring that dog up again later on this autumn. I'd like to hunt raccoons behind him some time."

Don nodded and waved. He leaned over Lance as the car started away. He stroked the great head gently, and the dog slowly thumped his tail on the floor before he closed his eyes.